I0621803

FOLLOW JEN

Follow her Newsletter
www.jengeiglejohnson.com

Jen's other published books

Dating the Duke
Time Travel: Regency man in NYC

Back To His Lordship
Regency Time Travel

The Nobleman's Daughter
Two lovers in disguise

Scarlet
The Pimpernel retold

A Lady's Maid
Can she love again?

Spun of Gold
Rumplestilskin Retold

Charmed by His Lordship
The antics of a fake friendship

Tabitha's Folly
Four over protective Brothers

To read Damen's Secret
The Villain's Romance

BACK TO HIS LORDSHIP

Clean Time Travel Regency Romance

JEN GEIGLE JOHNSON

San Diego, California 2020

Evaline Johansen eyed her hair dresser through the mirror. "Are you happy?"

The normally cute and spunky girl looked away, comb and scissors in hand. "Sure. As happy as anyone is, right?"

"I guess." Evaline sat in the styling chair, a colorful salon cape around her neck. "What I mean is, do you like what you do?" This woman had some of the most elite clients in Southern California. Most people had to book out six months at least. She must make a decent living by hair dresser standards.

"Yeah, sure." She flipped Eva's hair over to the other side of her head while she trimmed. "It stuck."

"I was just wondering." Eva had never had that satisfied feeling of finding her one place in life. Did she have a dream she worked at or hoped one day would happen? Not unless you counted her fascination with Jane Austen. But wishing you lived in a different time didn't count as a viable dream. She thought of her lists of things she'd love to do if she lived in the 1800's. Who did that, made goals for an imaginary 1800 life? Did she really want to live in a time with none of her modern conveniences, where women were treated as less smart, less capable and less knowledgable?

She checked her nails out of habit. They were perfect. Her hair would look just right when the stylist was finished. From the outside, Eva was put together. Plus, she'd completed college, and she made a stellar salary working at a successful marketing firm.

But was that her dream? She sighed.

Her phone rang from her purse, just behind *Persuasion*, her favorite Jane Austen. Relieved, Eva picked up the call. "Anna?" Her friend in England.

"What are you doing tomorrow?" No hello, no greeting, this was the way with Anna.

"Nothing noteworthy. Why? What's going on?" *Please let there be something amazing going on.*

"You need to come! A masquerade ball at Twickenham."

"Is that the estate near that Austen re-enactment resort?" She'd been to several re-enactments but never the largest and most famous.

"Twickenham. It's at the actual resort."

"Oh fun! When is it?"

"Two days. You need to hop on your jet asap."

"Don't they do these all the time? What's so important about this one?"

The pause for her to answer felt thick for a moment, but then Anna laughed. "No reason. I just think you'd love it. I'm bored. Come play with me."

She only needed another half-breath. "I'll be there tomorrow. Send a car?"

"Of course. I'm so happy you're coming. I'll have the guys there."

"Ooh, the Earls?" The idea of British nobility was still fascinating to Eva.

"Yes, and my man's coming too." The body builder, Trent, from the United States she'd been dating long distance for years.

"Are you two still together?"

"Depends on the day. But he's as yummy looking as ever so I can't leave him no matter what."

Eva smiled. They were the best couple. She wasn't sure what was holding them back. But maybe this trip she could figure it out, and find a yummy Englishman for herself. She giggled.

Her hairdresser smiled. "Fun plans?"

"I hope so." She closed her eyes, mentally packing during the rest of her hair appointment.

When she drove up the hill to her home on the bluff, the ocean spreading out to her front, she wondered why she wasn't satisfied with her life. Walking over her marble tile entry, trying to appreciate the floor length window view of the wide expanse of blue, she called her mom.

"Eva! How are you, dear? Thomas, say hi to Aunt Eva."

Her young nephew barely had time to say a quick hello before her mother was helping him build a block tower and then calling across the room to her father. Then the phone dropped on the floor and everything sounded muffled. Had she forgotten Eva? She waited for about a minute, hearing the laugher of children in the background, and then she gave up.

"Bye mom. I'll see you in a few weeks," she spoke to the empty house.

Her mother loved her, she assumed. She was given everything she could possibly need. But Eva's brother was married, had kids and lived just up the street. Everything seemed to be about them, their lives which were going at fifty miles an hour, and Eva always felt like a life waiting to happen to them.

Maybe she *was* a life waiting to happen. She shrugged. Not this week. She ignored the hurt that her mom had forgotten about her and started packing. She'd informed the pilot and everything was all set up for her to leave tonight. She'd sleep in her bed on the plane and awake refreshed and ready to go.

Once everything was in her bags, including her favorite enactment Regency gown with lovely shiny fabric and gorgeous lace. She'd added some extra touches herself. She did one more perusal around the room and her eyes fell on her old journal.

"Oh." She reached for it and opened to a well-worn page. "My bucket list."

She laughed at herself. For years she'd been collecting a list of things she would love to do if she lived during the Regency time period. It was silly, but it made her happy.

"Number one, visit Vauxhall Gardens, by boat. Number two, taste one of cook's biscuits. Number three, attend the opera. Number four, lead a true country dance." And so on. There was a page full of them. She knew that she'd never be able to really do any of her list, but it was fun to create, and now and then she'd add a new idea to the list. Maybe one day she'd write a book.

Carefully, she tucked the journal into her carryon and walked to the front door. The driver waited outside. Soon she was on her plane and heading across the water to England. She texted Anna. *On my way. Can't wait to see you.*

Anna responded with a dancing gif. Eva laughed and leaned her head back with a satisfied smile. There were few places she loved as much as England. And this masquerade ball sounded intriguing. She'd brought several things she could wear, but Anna had the closet to envy, and she was generous with her best pieces.

The flight went quickly. She slept and read. Eva just finished the confrontation with Lady Catherine De Bourgh and Miss Elizabeth in her well-read copy of *Pride and Prejudice*, when the captain announced they were preparing to land. She smiled and tucked her favorite classic up next to her journal in her carryon.

She descended the stairs of her jet, security and customs already taken care of, and hopped into Anna's car.

"Welcome back to England, Evaline." Anna's driver had worked for her for as long as Anna could remember.

"Thank you, Joseph."

"I understand we are meeting Miss Anna at the house?"

"Yes, that is my understanding as well."

The drive across country went by quickly as well. She dozed in and out of awareness and at last they were pulling in front of a lovely estate home. The rolling green of England stretched for miles in every direction and if she looked far enough to the right, the walls of Twickenham rose up above the treeline. She couldn't have limited the stretch of her smile if she wanted to. A vacation full of real British nobles, a masquerade in a noble ancient house, time with one of her dearest friends. Eva hoped the time away would help her figure out the direction of her life, figure out what she should be doing with herself. And maybe, she'd find someone worth spending time with. Was it too much to ask for a good guy, good manners, a ready smile and lots of fun?

Maybe.

Anna's butler opened the door. "Ah, Miss Evaline. We've been expecting you. You'll find Miss Anna—"

"Eva!" Anna came forward with both hands out. "Everything will be twice as wonderful now that you're here."

They kissed cheeks and Eva thanked Simmons, the butler, for directing her things upstairs.

"You'll be in the corner bedroom. It has a lovely view of the grounds. Go freshen up. They'll bring up a tray for you."

"I love the way you live. I keep trying to explain to my parents we overpay our servants to do less work." Anna laughed and Eva enjoyed the perfectly British high-class sound.

Eva made her way upstairs. Her windows overlooked the lovely green lawns and hedgerows and rose gardens of Anna's estate. England stretched out in every direction and she drank it in like she was home. Maybe she was home. Could she move across the ocean and set up a new life there? Her mother might not even notice. Her throat pinched at the thought but she pushed it away. Eva didn't have much going on that could compete with grandkids. That was perfectly understandable.

Sort of.

One of Anna's capable staff dropped off a tray on the table in her adjoining sitting room. She settled in with a variety of small sandwiches, cookies, and of course, tea. Anna had remembered her affinity for a particular herbal blend and she smiled as she brought it close to her mouth as the spicy smells filled her nose. "MMM."

A soft tap on the door and then Anna's head peeking in made her smile.

"Might I come in? I have someone I'd like you to meet."

"Of course." Eva stood.

Anna and a lovely woman who looked similar stepped into the room. Where Anna was light, this new woman was dark in hair. Her skin was a lovely pale creamy tone, but the shapes of their faces, the set of their mouths was remarkably similar.

"This is Bethany Lichfield."

Eva stepped forward. "I'm so happy to meet you. Eva Johansen. Are you two sisters?"

They shared a look, and Eva was immediately intrigued by the secretive smile that passed between them. Anna laughed, lightly, "Not sisters, but a relation, certainly."

Eva nodded, unsure what to think about that response but she gestured to her table. "Come, they've brought up way more than I could ever eat."

The three sat to take tea and refresh themselves together.

Bethany leaned forward. "Okay, what is on the plan for tonight? Are you going to bring that yummy Earl, what's his name? Lord Danbury?"

"Yes, they'll all come, Tindly, Boxby and Danbury, but I would think you'd be asking about Dr. Charles Smithy.

"Oh!" She fanned herself. "Darcy himself. Yes, will he be coming?"

"If I tell him you're here it might give him some motivation. After finishing his doctorate, the man spends more time with his intellectual friends, but we can still steal him away now and then."

They laughed and talked about all the local gossip, the royal ins and outs— Eva drank it in like nectar. She knew it might be somewhat frivolous, but she couldn't help but be caught up in the life of the royals, the fascinating manner in which they lived and were thought of. Anna, who was from an ancient noble family herself, replaced her tea cup. "And everyone's talking about who the dukes will marry. It's the talk of every paper, has been for months. It has their mother in a tizzy. I'm sure she'll welcome the day they've both settled down with proper and titled Englishwomen."

"And if they marry outside the nobility?" Eva wondered what kind of scandal that would cause.

"I think she's more open to such a plan. These next few years will be exciting ones in that area, I'm sure."

"And helpful because it might keep the press away from your lot."

"Exactly." Anna dabbed her face. "And now, shall we talk about tonight?"

They discussed the various clubs and places to dine until Eva was dizzy with excitement. "And I need to finalize my costume for the masquerade. Will you be coming, Bethany?"

Her face turned more solemn. "I'm uncertain. A part of me knows I should, but the other part wants to continue on as I have without a care."

What an odd response, as though the masquerade were an unpleasant task. But before she could ask further questions, Anna squealed and showed them a selfie from the Earl of Danbury.

As Eva laughed with the two of them and planned her vacation full of nothing important, she knew that very easily she could get blissfully lost in this life.

❧ 2 ❧

A London private ball 1818

Lord Oliver Hereford nearly spewed the lemonade from his mouth. "Keep your voice down."

"Is she not the one you've been pining after for an introduction?" Lord Castlebury widened his eyes in a ridiculous, overly innocent expression.

"I might attempt to secure an introduction, yes, but I don't see how your caterwauling about the woman to everyone nearby will help me win the respect of the woman's family or more importantly, hers."

"Are you seeking respect, then?" Lord Castlebury grinned. "If I'd known that was the intention, I might have limited my cups to only two."

His friends had been in their cups from the start of the evening and much to the hostess' chagrin, only mildly useful as guests at her ball. Lady Almston may never invite them to her home again. Though Oliver had kept himself in check, his friends were practically useless dance partners and created more of a disturbance than anything.

Perhaps he'd outgrown them. He'd certainly learned to keep matters most important to himself. But he enjoyed his friends. They were loyal to a fault and made endless social engagements bearable.

However, not tonight. Tonight he wanted to try his hand at actually securing the affections of a woman. And his set could be a hindrance more than anything. A distraction was in order. "We playing cards tonight?"

"If we keep the stakes low." Lord Tillsdale had lost a significant amount of his monthly allowance last week in a ridiculous bet against the Duke of Ramsbury.

"Speak of the devil." Oliver indicated the duke and his wife should join them.

"I don't recall speaking of him."

Oliver laughed and clapped him on the shoulder. "You didn't need to."

The duke and duchess of Ramsbury bowed and curtseyed and then the duke winked. "I imagine you'd like to win back some of your blunt…"

Lord Tillsdale huffed and said, "Not tonight. Tonight, the stakes are low. Or I'm out."

"Sounds fair enough." He whispered something in his wife's ear. And the smile she returned to him stole Oliver's breath. The love match his friend the Duke of Ramsbury shared with his wife was something Oliver had thought only existed in books. But when he saw evidence of their great caring day after day, he was motivated to seek out something for himself, not simply a mere amiability but a burning intensity between them. And when he'd determined that goal to be his lot in a marriage search, he became troubled at his friends' behavior. If only they could all be caught together in a game of cards while he went about the business of introductions and making new friendships.

The world seemed to align to grant his wishes. The duchess stepped forward and placed a hand on his arm. "Would you mind an escort for a refreshment while my husband shows mercy on these other gents in a game of chance?"

His eyes shot up to the duke's, who smiled warmly at his wife. Oliver nodded and led her away, tipping his head at the men who all had varying degrees of hidden sympathy in their expressions.

Once out of earshot, she whispered. "Now, let's get you those introductions."

He nearly stumbled. "What? How could you—"

"Never mind that. His grace and I have been talking. And we are going to help you. Now, who is the first one? A Lady Rose-meade, if I'm not mistaken?"

He swallowed. "The very one. Might I thank you? I admit to being uncertain how to go about such a thing."

She shook her head. "And you, raised here."

Her words were sometimes curious. He didn't always follow her train of thought, but if she was going to do him the great service of helping ease the way into meeting a proper woman, then he would follow along. They approached Lady Rosemeade, her reddish curls bouncing against her face as she turned to laugh at something the young lady on her right was saying. When she turned back, her laugh cut short and her eyes widened as she fumbled with her fingers. Not the best beginning. But perhaps she was nervous.

They bowed and curtseyed, and Oliver asked her for a dance without bumbling. He considered it a great coup when he led her out on the floor without so much as a glitch in their interactions.

As they waited for their turn down the line, he searched her face. Would they feel anything when they touched? Would the beginnings of a romance begin in that very dance? She returned his gaze with a somewhat bold one of her own. "I've enjoyed the season."

"Oh, yes, I as well. Better this one than last." He smiled. And wanted to kick himself. All clever thought left the moment he felt compelled to be clever. As if the very act of attempting anything memorable would stifle his best efforts.

"It's my first so I don't have much to compare."

"Oh, I know. I've been hoping for an introduction since I first saw you." That sounded way too desperate, but her face colored a charming pink.

"Have you? I'm pleased we've managed one then." Her responses were safe, calculated, bland. As were most of the proper new debutantes of the town. The more brazen set were perhaps more fun, but he'd heard, not the marrying kind. Could he begin to feel something for this pretty little red head if they never spoke of more than the pleasantries? He wasn't sure, but he decided he must give them time.

When it was their turn to scoot down the middle of the row of people, his hands cradled hers and he gazed into her eyes. She smiled at him. He smiled back. But that was the end of it. He felt nothing. They circled the couples at their sides and came back together before returning to their positions, facing each other in line. Her pretty demeanor was heightened by the flush of exertion, and he vowed to ask her to accompany him to the lemonade after.

"Tell me about your family, your estate." She surprised him with a question, a personal one.

"I come from the north of England in a lovely estate and grounds that border the ocean."

Her eyes lit with interest. And though he was pleased to see it, he wondered at her sincerity.

"Do you enjoy the sea?"

"Oh yes, there is something so lovely about the water, and the waves."

She'd hit upon his very interest. "Yes, the sound of them crashing on shore helps me think."

"Oh?"

"Yes, I wander the shoreline when a problem hits me, something I'm unable to muddle through on my own..."

Her attention had wandered to her friends waiting her return on the side of the floor. He stopped talking and she didn't ask him to continue. Perhaps no lemonade after all.

As the music ended and everyone in the line had their turn to dance, he led her back to her friends, bowing to her and thanking her.

The duchess showed back up at his side. "Did you ask to call?"

"Well, no, she seemed rather bored."

"Everyone's bored their first dance. Ask her."

He turned around and the eyes of all her friends widened as he returned. "I was wondering if I might call on you this week?"

She curtseyed. "Why, yes, of course."

He nodded, then led the duchess away.

"Excellent. Now, Ollie." She was the only one in the world he allowed to call him Ollie. "Be more interesting."

"But she's not interesting."

"And the other thing I was going to add. Be more interested."

His mouth fell open. Then he closed it. "That's brilliant."

She tipped her head. "I wish I'd thought of it myself. But one key to winning friends and influencing people is to be interested—*in them*. I threw in the 'interesting' part because I think you're a perfectly lovely person with so much to offer, but only the guys see your more flavorful side. Show a sense of humor, stand a little closer, make her smile and laugh, and give her something to tease and intrigue her sensibilities even long after you're gone."

He watched her face with a growing fascination. "And I might win someone over."

"Most definitely."

He held up a finger and spoke closer to her ear. "I don't want a woman to pretend to like me. I am looking for a love match." He felt his own face burn while he said it.

"I understand, and those are the only kinds of matches I support."

"You do?"

"Certainly. This whole business of people marrying unhappily for all the wrong reasons does not sit well with me at all."

He nodded, finding her refreshingly odd. But he should be used to his friend's wife's antics by now. "I shall do my best."

Hopefully, his best would provide the beginnings of a love match between him and some as yet undetermined woman.

❧ 3 ❧

Eva whirled in her dress. It billowed out all around her. When she stopped again in front of the mirror, the folds of fabric hung in a respectable straight line down to the floor. The brilliant blue made her smile. It shimmered like the water in a windy day, like streams of sunlight sparkling off the water. She loved the water. Perhaps on this trip, she'd find her way to the coast somehow. Brighton. Dover. Bath. Or some of the northern cities. They felt more undiscovered, more rugged.

She reached for her mask. Wearing her long white gloves, she felt awkward as she tried to pinch her fingers around the small purse. Finally, she moved out into the hall and descended the stairs, ready for the ball to begin.

Going to a ball in England. That should definitely be added to her Regency bucket list.

At the base of the stairwell, Lord Danbury looked up and then looked again, and she smiled. "Hello."

She moved forward reaching out a hand. "Well, hello to you."

His deep tones and lovely accent flowed over her. She could hear these men talk all day.

"Are we all almost ready?"

"I can say with certainty that you are." He stepped away to admire her. "You look lovely." He was a handsome man, standing taller than most with broad shoulders, thick arms, and a strong jaw line. She could totally get into a guy like him even without his enticing British title and manner of speaking.

"And so do you. What are you dressed as?" Sometimes at these balls, the mask was only part of the costume. Many came with a theme.

"I wanted to come as Zorro, but perhaps too expected, a man in a mask, everyone is Zorro, you know?" he stood taller. "So now, I'm simply, Lord Danbury in a mask."

She laughed. "It works. You look like Lord Danbury in a mask."

"And you are going to turn every head." His eyes showed interest. She was surprised to see it. He'd always seemed to be more interested in the conquest, in the party scene, but something about his expression hinted that she might hear from him again.

"Well, thank you."

Anna descended, looked between the two of them, and her smile grew. "We're waiting on the others."

As if on cue, the doorbell rang and the butler opened it. The rest of the guys and Bethany stepped into the entry.

Dr. Charles Smithy, Lord Boxby, and Lord Tindly were equally impressive, filling the space with a massive amount of handsome power. Her heart skipped just standing next to them all. But she also knew their type. She'd been around power hungry American businessmen her whole life. Her major at the university was full of them, her father's friends and sons were the same. Her own brother and his friends gave the same vibe. But these men were impressive no matter how accustomed she was to their levels of testosterone. And she looked forward to arriving with them to this party. Part of her wanted to watch the heads of every lady in the room turn to look at them. She laughed.

Anna joined her. "Who's ready?"

They turned to climb in the now waiting limo. Eva sat pressed between Lord Danbury and Dr. Smithy.

"How's your research?"

Lord Danbury groaned. "Don't ask him."

"Why not? She wants to know. I sense an equally intelligent mind and someone who appreciates good research."

She laughed. "And I just really want to know how it's going." She shrugged. "But we can talk about it another time."

"Yes, thank you." Lord Danbury stretched his arm along the back of their seats. "Would you save a dance for me?"

"Of course."

"In fact, I might stay close..."

"No, you can't be hovering about like her body guard." Anna scoffed. "Give her some space and enjoy your dance when it comes."

Eva smiled. "Both ideas are welcome."

"Understood. How about we meet for the third dance after we arrive, over by the front pillars?"

She nodded. "It's a plan. And thank you."

The car pulled in the front drive of Twickenham. The estate was situated a mere two miles from Anna's home.

"It's lovely." Eva craned her head to see out the window. The home was large, larger than she expected. And she was surprised to see gargoyles along the roof line. "How interesting. I'm having a difficult time placing the architecture. What year was this house built?"

Lord Danbury nodded. "Most people have the same trouble. It stands outside of time, really. So many pieces from different eras make up the whole. I see something different every time I look at it."

Eva thought that extraordinarily strange, but as she examined the house again, she noticed the gables and the interesting stone work, none of which she'd seen before. The gargoyles were still there but not taking up the whole of her attention.

"Fascinating. Like it's—timeless."

They approached the house, and the butler let them all in. He dipped his head to Anna. Music blared from further into the house. Anna laughed. "Aunt Nellie thinks this place is a club now."

Dr. Smithy joined her. "Let's go check it out."

They hurried toward the sound and Eva was left wondering what aunt of Anna's lived here. Aunt Nellie? She'd never heard of her, and that sounded strangely common and even overly familiar for Anna's crowd. They entered the ballroom and Eva gasped in happy surprise. "This is beautiful!"

"Better put your mask on." Lord Boxby lowered his.

"Oh right, thank you." She slid the mask over her eyes, resting on her nose. It stretched by band to the back of her head and she could see through the holes for her eyes.

"You look stunning." Lord Danbury bowed. "Until the third?"

As soon as he turned away, Anna clung to her side. "What's this?"

"I don't know. He's acting maybe interested?"

"You know what kind of player he is."

"I know. But maybe this is different?"

Anna shrugged. "I'd be happy to see such a thing occur for him and you."

They moved to the center of the floor, the other men of their party dispersing through the crowds and a new group joining them. The beat was loud, pulsing and easy to dance to but odd in their setting. Eva waved her hands in the air and bounced around in happy abandon.

When it came time to meet Lord Danbury for her dance, she moved toward the beverages and spun slowly in happy anticipation. It wasn't every day that she was feeling interest from someone so celebrated. Not only was he titled but he did a lot of work for local hospitals and to support educational opportunities and growth in England's universities.

But the start of the next song came and went and still no Lord Danbury at her side. She gave it thirty more seconds into the fourth song, grabbed a drink, and made her way out into the cooler hallways. Lord Danbury was obviously not into her. Perhaps Lord Boxby or any of the others might be entertaining a bit later.

The air was much fresher and the sounds muffled as she exited the ballroom. The further away she walked, the more loathe she was to return. Eyeing an inviting turning staircase, she hurried towards it instead.

As soon as her foot touched the bottom stair, she felt compelled to reach the top, one foot after another pushing faster and farther and more incessantly until she reached the top landing. She wandered down the halls, peering into doors, observing the typical rooms of the English gentry.

She climbed the stairwell at the end of the hall, up and up to the seventh floor where she entered a large portrait gallery, taking up most of the floor.

Ooh, she loved art, especially portraits. The people in the portraits seemed to be from all walks of life and time periods. Many of them were obviously upper-class. But many were also in jeans, leggings, workout clothes, or ripped up farm hand material. And each one of them had an interesting expression. Some were smiling, but their eyes were full of surprise. Some were deadpan, but their mouth opened as if about to say something. Some were openly surprised. Some were caught mid motion even, which Eva found interesting as she'd never seen a painting look more like an action shot. And some, amusingly enough, looked just like selfies. She wondered if someone had turned a selfie into a painting for fun. Perhaps it was all the rage in modern Britain.

A woman approached on her left. Regal in her bearing, cheerful in her countenance, Eva waited for her to be near enough, and then she smiled. "Hello."

"Are you enjoying our portrait gallery?" Her white hair gleamed in the candle light. Her blue eyes flashed and this seemed odd to Eva, but there was something ancient about her, as though she belonged in this timeless and ancient house.

"Yes, very much. I find some of the poses fascinating and the talent at capturing accuracy very welcome."

"I'm happy to hear it. I do all the work myself."

"Oh, that's incredible. I'm so happy to be able to meet you. I'm Eva Johansen." She held out her hand to shake.

The woman took hers and Eva felt an interesting buzz of energy go through her. "And I'm Aunt Nellie."

"Oh! Anna's aunt. Then I'm doubly glad to meet you. I'm staying with her right now."

Aunt Nellie smiled, amused at something. "I'm not really anyone's aunt, but the name has stuck, and there we have it."

They made their way down the far wall of the room until a portrait ahead caught her eye. The blue of a gown seemed strikingly familiar. She hurried forward, leaving Aunt Nellie behind her. When she saw the mask on the woman, the exact same mask on her own face, she ripped it off and whirled around to face Aunt Nellie. "How odd!"

But no one was behind her, the portrait room now completely empty except for herself. How doubly odd. She turned back to the picture, stepping as close as she dared. The blue was the exact same shade. The dress hung precisely as it did on herself, and her hair was lifted up in the same style with precisely the same curl handing down at the side of her face. Her breathing came faster. She swallowed, feeling somewhat dizzy. But how could Aunt Nellie have painted her in the exact outfit she was wearing when she herself didn't even know what outfit that would be? She'd gone through at least three this morning and rummaged through Anna's entire closet. "This cannot be."

And yet it was. She wished she had a phone to take a picture. No one would believe such a thing had happened. Perhaps it wasn't paint at all. Perhaps just digitally manufactured to look like paint and they hurriedly hung portraits of all the guests? She reached out her finger to run along the blue of her dress. But the texture under her finger felt as authentic as any painting. Before she could analyze it any further, the world whirled around her. Everything went white except for the sparkling snowfall of a glitter like substance. A magically cheerful giggle echoed in the air around her and then it spun in a dizzying madness faster and faster until at once, everything stopped.

She reached out for something, still seeing nothing.

"Are you quite alright?" A man. With a brilliant voice.

She gasped and then opened her eyes.

The world had returned to full color, portraits hung all around, though they seemed aged, different. Her own portrait looked the same. The room at least was not spinning. But she was not alone.

A man stood in front of her. Tall, dressed deliciously in the style of the men in Jane Austen's time, breeches and all. He stepped closer. "Might I be of assistance?"

His voice was deep and charming, the accent British, as expected, but with an air of finery, of gentility, she found missing in her group even. He held himself in a straight backed manner, his expression revealing nothing, his stance the practiced ease of those truly comfortable with their manner of dress and lifestyle. But his eyes. They sparkled with intrigue, interest and, she was fascinated to see, a hint of rebellious adventure.

Without telling it to, her eyebrow rose in challenge. "Assistance? I don't know, are you free a little later?" She laughed, surprised at her own courage.

But he tilted his head, eyeing her as though to attempt to understand. "And what might you need a little later on?"

She stopped laughing, realizing that the man was entirely devoid of a sense of humor, perhaps. "Oh, no, I was...um." She looked up into his face and he eyed her a moment longer, then his cheeks colored. "Good heavens. You didn't mean. Later, as in, perhaps I might be available for a dalliance of some kind?"

His shock and surprise at her joke puzzled her.

Then he laughed the kind of laugh one attempts to hold in but simply cannot. "And now I'm finally understanding you were in jest."

When he finally stopped and wiped his eyes, she stepped away.

"No, don't be alarmed. I'm usually much quicker to understand such things, but typically I don't hear that manner of humor from a lady. Usually it's coming from the men of my acquaintance, not that I mind. It was refreshingly candid. And you are welcome to try out such humor on me again, if you like." He waited, watching her with a newfound delight in his eyes.

If he wasn't the most attractive man she'd ever seen, she might have steered clear of such an odd person, but something had jiggled her brain a moment ago and she did need a bit of assistance perhaps.

"I don't know if I have anything quite so witty."

And then he bowed. "I'm Lord Oliver Hereford. At your service."

Because she didn't know what else to do, she curtseyed in response. "And I'm Lady Eva." Where had that come from? Lady Eva? But before she could respond, shouts sounded in the hall. He ushered her around the corner into an alcove. "Hush now. If you stay quiet no one will discover us."

Too confused for words, she watched the urgency in his face as he spoke. Perhaps she'd done something odd to her own brain when she touched that painting. Perhaps it wasn't of herself after all. Once the sound of voices had passed, he looked down into her face. "I would apologize for the closeness of our situation, but I find this is…nice."

He smelled fantastic, filling her nose, lungs, head with as strong an essence of pure man as she'd ever known. She fought everything inside her that urged her hand to rise up and rest on his chest. Instead, she smiled and said, "Yes, it is." At a complete loss to understand what had just happened, what was going on inside her head, she was afraid to say much of anything.

"I think we are free to return to the gallery. Perhaps you should go and find your chaperone."

She nodded.

"And I shall hurry out ahead of you so no one suspects we have been here alone."

She nodded again, totally not following.

But then he raised her hand to his mouth and pressed his lips in between her knuckles. "It has been my pleasure Lady Eva. I hope to see much more of you." The intense sincerity of his eyes astounded her. She couldn't have moved if she'd wanted to.

"I as well." Her words came out in a sort of ragged rasping breathy sound. But he turned and left before she could repeat herself.

She waited for half a breath and then shook her head. "As if it matters that we're found alone together?" She wondered if he still lived by the rules in her Regency era romance novels? Was there a faction of the nobility who held to those thoughts? She'd have to ask Anna if that were the case.

She left her spot and rounded the corner to an empty portrait gallery once again. Making her way back to the painting of herself, she wanted to study it more. She stopped in front of the image. But first, her finger. Something about this whole encounter felt other worldly and she had to test the finger touch one more time to prove herself wrong.

Before she reached out her finger, another couple joined her. She in Regency dress and he dressed in the same breeches. Eva found this curious. So, she left the room, determined to see if more people had arrived in this particular costume and, she admitted, to see if she might find Lord Hereford again. She had not forgotten the feel of the pressure from his mouth on her hand. And like a crazed teenager, she wanted to stand close enough to embrace again.

As she descended the stairs and walked out along the stairway banister, she sucked in her breath. Everything was the same, but different. The chandelier flickered with candles aflame. The guests were all in Regency attire, the house felt unaccountably cold. "No." She backed away. Something had shaken her mind, disturbed her thinking. She returned to the portrait gallery at a run, back to the image of herself. And she held her finger up, running it along the paint ridges of the blue in her dress.

Once again the world spun, white, glitter falling all around. And when it stopped, she found herself not even waiting for the dizziness to pause. She ran from the room, down the stairs and out across the balcony. She breathed out a long exhale of relief. The lights were electric. The people were dressed in modern ballgowns and tuxedos, the temperature had returned and there was a lovely modern smell of dinner wafting up to her.

She descended the stairs, anxious to find Anna and ask her all about this new lord, Lord Hereford.

❧ 4 ❧

Oliver waited at the bottom of the stairs for Lady Eva to join him for much longer than any other person would have. But she never descended. Many climbed the stairs talking of the portrait gallery. Some talked of journeys, travels, as though they would be doing something more than merely touring the house. Some were tearful, as though saying goodbye. Not as many came back down as went up, he noticed after thirty minutes when a gentleman descended without the woman at his side.

After an hour, and then a quarter more, he drifted away. Perhaps there was a back stairwell she'd used. Perhaps he'd now missed her altogether.

Hurrying back into the ballroom, his eyes scanned the guests. Her dress would be easy to spot, such a brilliant blue was not often seen among the ladies. But after a moment, he was sure she was not to be found in the overcrowded room. And the longer he looked, the longer he waited, the more his anticipation grew. He'd never encountered such a woman. Never felt so drawn to one as he was her. The feeling of interest, of potential, was so strong with her, he had to immediately understand where and how to find her again.

His eyes found her grace. She was surrounded by the duke and their friends. When he reached her side, he murmured. "I've found her."

She immediately turned. "Have you?"

"Yes, she's incredible."

"My. Well, who is it?"

"I don't know."

She eyed him a moment more, then her eyes sharpened. "You've never seen her before?"

"No."

"What was her name?"

"Lady Eva."

"And we don't know anyone by that name."

He shook his head.

The duke, who had taken a sudden interest in the conversation, leaned forward. "Were you by chance up on the seventh floor?"

His eyes widened. "Yes! Tell me. What do you know?"

They exchanged glances and then the duke said, "Nothing. I was just wondering."

Oliver nearly growled in frustration. They so obviously knew something. What was it about the seventh floor? Had they witnessed his meeting of Lady Eva? Or seen her descend? Or perhaps they'd talked to her? But they turned away and began talking with a couple on their other side, and Oliver was left to stew alone.

A pair of women passed, giggling into their hands causing him to miss Lady Eva even more. Something about her seemed more real than the others. And he doubted very much that she ever giggled into her hands. But what did he know about her, really? He closed his eyes, remembering their huddled moments in the alcove. She had been deliciously close, almost in his arms. He had sensed the adventure stirring in her, seen the daring in her eyes.

Then Lady Rosemeade came into his periphery and he told himself, forced movement in his feet, commanded himself to move in her direction and have a conversation.

The music started for a new set and so he bowed. "Might I have another set with you?"

She curtseyed. "Of course." Again, the perfect politeness, the emotional restraint. Did she care for him? Was there a surge of energy making her head swim? He would never know. But he led her out onto the floor, and they began an interminably long quadrille. How had he not paid attention to the music and the gathering dancers when he'd asked her? What if Lady Eva showed herself in the middle of the dance?

But Lady Rosemeade turned humorous, and he found himself enjoying the dance more than he thought. For a moment, he forgot he was meant to be looking for the mysterious Lady Eva and enjoyed Lady Rosemeade instead.

When it was their turn to circle, she approached him and they linked hands. "I've heard there's to be a balloon at Vauxhall Wednesday."

"Is there! Now that would be something to see."

She circled around him and by the time she returned, he smiled. "Would you like to go? Make an afternoon of it?"

"Yes. I'd love that." Her smile turned up in a demure half lift, her eyes looked down at the floor, and she became the perfect picture of propriety.

He vowed to disturb her perfectly poised demeanor. Did she have passion? Did she care for anything deeply, intently? His thoughts again returned to Lady Eva, who he had no doubt carried a fiery burning passion about any number of topics. How did he know such a thing? He wasn't certain, but he'd be willing to bet all his next earnings at Tattersall's to find out.

THE MEN SAT AROUND A TABLE AT WHITE'S, EACH IN A quandary. Lord Tillsdale swirled his brandy, frowning at it so sternly that Oliver began to wonder if he'd throw his cup against the wall. "Do you suppose they talked? All our mums?"

Lord Biddle shrugged. "They might have, but what does it matter? Here we are, strapped tight, our allowances limited."

"Unless we show signs that we're taking life seriously." Lord Tillsdale frowned.

Lord Biddle downed his drink. "And how's a man supposed to do that?"

"Well for one, my mum says I have to make a real attempt to find a woman to marry." Lord Castlebury shook his head. "Which I am loathe to do."

"And that's not the half of it...curtailing the tables, horses, and all the hells. What else is a man to do in this town?" Lord Tillsdale took a long drink then held up his finger. "And don't be telling me the opera."

"No one says you have to go to the opera." Oliver laughed inside at the men, secretly pleased they might present themselves in a more respectable manner.

"But it's implied, isn't it?" Lord Tillsdale waved over another drink. "Keep a woman happy, show some serious attention to someone, and I'll get an increase in my allowance."

"And what is the matter with that? A little feminine attention would be welcome." Oliver eyed them all with hope, but they scoffed or grunted or disagreed in one manner or another.

Oliver found the whole lot of them pathetic. For years they'd been his friends. Why now were they suddenly resolute reprobates with zero to recommend them but the ability to make a gentleman laugh?

He could hardly stand their presence, so he stood with the pretense of refilling his cup somewhere else. The Duke of Ramsbury entered the room and Oliver met him at the door.

"Just the man I'd hoped to see," Oliver said.

"And you are who I came to see." His gaze flickered over their group. "Might we have a moment alone?"

"Please."

"As good as all that?"

"About as terrible as you imagine. Their allowances have been cut. Their card days are over, and they've been commanded to find a woman to marry."

The duke's raised eyebrows made Oliver laugh. "Well now, all of that sounds like responsible adulthood."

Oliver dipped his head in agreement then they moved to a table in the corner. The others had yet to look their way. Oliver gave them ten minutes to take notice.

The duke moved closer to Oliver. "Have you found the mysterious Lady Eva?"

"No. My mother has not heard of her, thinks I made her up so she'll stop hounding me to marry. No one seems to know a Lady Eva."

"And you're certain she's not making up a name or title just to impress you only to run?"

The thought had never occurred to Oliver, but as he considered such a thing, he shook his head. "I can't imagine it of her. But I suppose all things are possible."

"And now I have a bit of a strange question to ask of you. In the portrait gallery, did you see a picture of yourself?"

"What?"

"A portrait, of you."

"No. I didn't. But when I met Lady Eva, she was standing in front of a portrait of herself in the precise outfit she had on that evening." He leaned forward, staring at the duke. "What precisely is going on?"

The duke's eyes sparkled with mystery. "I'll just tell you that if she has a portrait of herself in that gallery, that's either a very good sign for you or a terrible one."

"Be specific, man."

He ran a hand through his hair. "It's dashed difficult to explain to a person. But I think you should be at the next ball on the full moon at Twickenham."

"Again? You think she'll be there?"

He held up his hands. "I don't know, but I think she might. And while you're there, put your attentions on the portrait gallery. There might be a few people you'll be surprised to see."

"Like yourself."

The duke nodded.

"And the duchess?"

He nodded again.

"What is it? Some sort of marriage arranger?"

"Hardly." He snorted. "For many months I hated that house and what it could do to a person's life."

A strange ominous kneading began in Oliver's gut.

"But sometimes it works out splendidly. Just come. It's worth it to see, isn't it? Besides, Jane and I will be there as well."

Oliver's suspicions were conflicting and powerful, but he nodded anyway. The possibility he might run into the fascinating Lady Eva again was too alluring to resist. "I'll be there."

5

As soon as Eva searched the entire ballroom and lower floors, the sickening realization that her Lord Hereford was nowhere in sight grew in her at the same momentum as the realization that she wanted him in her life. She climbed back up the stairs and walked again through the portrait gallery, careful not to touch any of the paintings.

She wasn't sure what she was looking for particularly, but she searched each face until at last she came to a familiar face: Anna. Years younger and dressed in Regency attire. She was surrounded by a room full of women and as Eva looked closer, she recognized Bethany. The ladies looked similar, like sisters.

Eva couldn't understand this room. Did Anna know her picture was up here? She moved down the row, wondering if she knew anyone else in the portraits. She stopped in front of one that looked incredibly like an associate who she hadn't seen in years. Jane Sullivan, smiling, wearing a Regency dress. She'd published some ground-breaking research about women in the nineteenth century and then all but disappeared from the professional world. Her parents were rumored to be living in Italy and no one could ever give her more information about the elusive Jane.

Something otherworldly, maybe suspicious, was going on in this room and Eva wanted to get to the bottom of it. Bare minimum, she needed to warn Anna and Bethany. She hurried from the room and nearly ran down Dr. Smithy.

"Oh, my apologizes. Are you alright, Evaline?"

"You can call me Eva." She steadied under his strong hands and then stepped away. "Do you know where Anna and Bethany are?"

"Yes, I believe they're dancing."

"Okay." She looked away from him and then back. Perhaps he'd have a thought about what she should do. "Come in here. Might I show you something?"

"Certainly. I've never been in this room before."

"Have you been to Twickenham often?"

"No, just once when I was doing my research. A colleague of mine and I were here doing a Jane Austen re-enactment with the hopes we could see some original research, letters and things that belonged, ironically, to Anna."

"What? Really. So, what happened?"

"My colleague won. Jane was incredible at finding her way into the most remarkable situations."

"Jane? Jane Sullivan?"

"The very one! Do you know her?"

"I do. Though I haven't seen her in years."

"Nobody has."

"Do you know why?"

His expression was strange but guarded. "No."

"Come in. I want you to see this." She led him into the room and took him first to Jane's portrait.

"Ah there she is. I always did admire that one." He reached forward as though to touch her face.

"No! Don't touch."

"I wasn't going to touch. I'm a researcher, remember?"

"No, it's not that." She felt her face heat in embarrassment. "Something happened."

"What?"

"Follow me." She led him back down the other side of the room and stopped in front of her portrait. Only it wasn't there. "What? Wait. Where did it go?"

"Where did what go?"

"Right here. In this spot was a portrait of me."

"Of you?" His eyebrow raised in skepticism. Eva would have thought it quite charming were it not directed at her.

"Yes, of me. Why do you keep making me repeat myself?"

"I'm just not seeing the portrait, that's all."

She frowned and didn't know what else to do or say. She wanted to walk up and down the gallery searching every portrait until she found the one with herself again, but Dr. Smithy was starting to walk out of the room. "I should have mentioned before now, Lord Danbury was looking for you earlier."

Irritation simmered. "Oh, was he?"

Dr. Smithy didn't notice her only partly suppressed annoyance. "Yes, he said he's looking for that dance you promised him."

If he'd been where he said he would be, they could have danced...she stopped her train of thought. And she never would have met Lord Hereford. But where was the guy?

"Shall we?" Dr. Smithy held his arm out for her to take. She placed her mask back on her face and took his arm while they descended the stairs and made their way back into the ballroom.

As soon as they entered the room and she dropped her hand from Dr. Smithy's sleeve, a man approached and bowed to her. "May I have this dance?"

She nodded and performed an awkward curtsey in response. "Certainly." Something about him reminded her of Lord Hereford, and she was determined to find out more about him.

The music was slow and had somewhat of a waltz three beat. He took her into his arms, with one hand on her waist and the other holding her hand out to their side, leading her around the room in a manner she never had before.

"You're an excellent dancer!"

"Thank you. You're quite proficient yourself."

"I learned the waltz at a Regency retreat years ago, and I've practiced a bit now and then."

"And your instructors helped, undoubtedly."

"My instructors."

He led her around the room in such an expert manner she thought that perhaps he'd had dancing lessons and instructors himself.

"I was at Whites the other day, and they are placing bets on when the biddies at Almack's will allow the waltz in their hallowed walls."

"Almack's?" She half laughed, but he seemed authentic, sincere. She half felt like she was talking with an actor from a Regency enactment experience.

"But I think they'll allow anyone as soon as tomorrow if a duchess or other titled lady will begin."

She nodded. "Undoubtedly." Was she to play along with his charade? "And just where are you from?"

"I have an estate near Hertfordshire, but I spend more of my time in London off Grosvenor square."

"Hertfordshire, really?" She laughed. Could he not think of any locale more unique than the one where the Bennet family lived in *Pride and Prejudice*?

But he tipped his head and his mouth moved in a disapproving frown. "Have you a dislike for Hertfordshire?"

"Oh no, certainly not. I myself am from the lake country, Derbyshire to be exact, perhaps you've heard of it?"

"Naturally. I travel there often."

She stared at him, trying to make him break character, but he continued to move about the room, the perfect gentlemen, likely thinking her more and more odd the longer they talked. But she was not the odd one. He was most certainly living and acting as though he were in the Regency time period. Perhaps just to add authenticity to his costume.

"I see we've dispensed with the masks." She smiled.

"As so many others have as well. I find them tedious."

"I agree. It's so much more difficult to see as well, and I like to be acquainted with my dance partner."

"I do apologize for our lack of introduction, but Aunt Nellie assured me it is the manner in which they do things here." He stood taller. "I am Sir Jacob."

"And I am Lady Eva." She played along.

"The pleasure is mine."

"Is Aunt Nellie your aunt?"

He eyed her again. "Certainly not."

"Then why address her so?"

Confusion clouded his expression, and he didn't seem to know how to answer. So she spared him the trouble. "I find her charming, but I couldn't get a clear answer from her about her name."

He nodded. "Just so. And things are dashed strange in this time period. I've felt better since drinking her tea, but the lights. Look at them."

Eva lifted her head up to see a glittering, magnificent chandelier and didn't quite know how to respond. "Hmm." Then she remembered her own fascination. "Yes. I do know what you mean. Were you by any chance upstairs in the portrait gallery?"

"Of course."

The dance ended and he escorted her back to the side of the floor when another gentleman asked her to dance. Her mind was still spinning from the last, but she curtseyed and said she would.

He talked in the same old-fashioned British manner as Lord Hereford and Sir Jacob. So she tried something different. "What happened last summer?"

"Last summer?" He frowned in confusion.

"Yes." She fumbled around in her thoughts. "In the house of Lords, how did they adjourn?"

"Oh, it was a difficult session. Everyone was still up in arms about Napoleon. He's on that dratted island you know, and there are some who think he should be executed." He pressed his lips together. "Beg your pardon for my abrupt manner of speaking."

"No, that's quite alright. Tell me, do you belong to Whites, Brooks, or Boodles?"

"Oh, Whites certainly. You wouldn't ever find me near that Whig establishment."

Interesting. Could it be a whole room full of men Aunt Nellie had hired to act as though they lived in the Regency time period?

"You're the first woman I've danced with tonight who's talked sense. Aunt Nellie told me most people wouldn't understand where I'm from, that I'd have to learn the new way of things, but I understand you just perfectly."

Pieces of information were coming together in a manner that fit, but they still puzzled her. "So, are you visiting for a time?"

"Time." He eyes turned wistful. "Apt way of expressing the process."

How frustrating to be on the cusp of understanding and yet not quite grasp something that felt important.

The dance ended and Anna approached. Eva thanked her partner and ran the remaining few steps to her friend. "What is wrong with everyone?"

"Wrong?" She turned to watch the man leave her side. Then she smiled. "Ah, you got a Regency one, didn't you?"

"Two, three even." She pulled her to the side of the room. "And what do you mean, a Regency one?"

"Well they're from all over. I danced with a few from the forties, the seventies even. That was an experience. I think he might have been high. But I most prefer the Regency men. They're so deliciously proper. It's fun to mess with their sensibilities."

Eva just shook her head over and over again, unsure what to say.

"You're driving me crazy. Stop shaking your head."

"But you can't be serious."

"I am perfectly serious. You should know. You went through your portrait today." She tapped her finger on her chin. "Though most don't return the same day. Did you arrange it that way? How long were you gone?"

"You are making no sense. At all."

"Let's go sit somewhere quiet." She led her down the hall, around a corner and into a library. The room was comforting, the smell of books, old books, washed over Eva and she felt a bit calmer. Nothing made sense, but at least there were still books in the world.

"Let's sit." Anna reached for her hand as they sat, then let it go. She shifted her weight.

"I saw your picture."

"Oh, you did?" Her smile warmed. "With all the Lichfield sisters."

"Bethany was there, too."

"Oh she was. You are so correct."

"And my portrait was there."

"Yes, naturally, or how else could you have jumped in time?"

"Jumped...in time?"

Anna searched her face in annoying amusement. "You must not have gone too far down the stairs."

"No, but the chandelier was different—candles. The people were all dressed Regency costume instead of just a few. And it was cold."

Anna shivered "That's what I remember most. It's always cold. And drafty."

"So, are you saying I stepped back in time?"

"You certainly did. Now tell me. Did you meet anyone?"

"Yes." Her face heated and the smile she tried to stifle in this confusing and serious conversation would not be stopped.

"Oh, you did! Spill. Tell me all about him."

"His name is Lord Hereford."

Her small gasp made Eva search her face.

"Do you know him?"

"No, I don't think so. Perhaps." She waved her hand around. "Continue."

"So, he was standing there in the portrait room after I almost passed out."

Anna smiled. "And?"

"And we talked. He was lovely. We hid in an alcove, like they do in all the books, and I've been missing him ever since."

A look of triumph filled Anna's face so much that Eva immediately leaned away in hesitation.

Unphased, Anna reached for her hands. "How much do you want to see him?"

"What do you mean?"

"What would you do if I told you there was a way to go back in time to see him? And it wasn't permanent. You could return at any full moon."

"Full moon, what? Now I know this is hokey."

"You saw the evidence. I'm just telling you what you saw."

Eva thought it through. "And you're saying if I touch my painting again, I'll go back in time and I can find him in the time where he lives?"

She bit her lip. "Usually."

"What do you mean, usually? It seems a bit of a risk if you can't guarantee when you come back."

"Aunt Nellie's almost always got it right. And she can fix whatever mess we all get up in."

"So *you've* done this?"

"I have. Often. Lately not as much because it gives me the worst headache...and I have Trent here." She smiled. "But it's perfectly lovely. You can go and stay in a time for as long as you like and come back as though you never left."

Eva leaned back on the sofa, her world reeling. She closed her eyes. "You're telling me this is for real?"

"Most certainly." A voice she might have recognized responded.

Eva opened one eye and then sat up when she saw Aunt Nellie. "I met a man. In the portrait gallery. Is Lord Hereford from a different time?"

"Yes."

"Can you send me to that time?"

"Probably. I rarely get it wrong by too many years."

Eva didn't think that was too encouraging. But she was intrigued. What could it hurt to try? She'd already had some kind of an experience she didn't feel qualified to explain. So how could it harm anyone were she to have another? "I'd like to try it, if I might?"

"I thought you'd say so." Aunt Nellie moved around the other side of her desk and lifted the portrait.

"There it is!"

"Yes."

"It's an incredible likeness."

"Thank you. I do take pride in these. A small masterpiece of its kind, really. Serves a purpose but might as well have beauty with the function. Now, if you could come forward. I'll need you to make contact with the portrait again."

"Ok." She looked back over her shoulder at Anna, only half believing what was about to happen. She reached her finger out and ran it along the blue of her dress then turned to wave goodbye to Anna as the world swirled around her.

❧ 6 ❧

Oliver felt a bit ridiculous, traveling out to Twickenham again to be there on the full moon so that he might see a mysterious lady he'd met for only a few minutes. But the ridiculousness of the situation could not cloud or dim the intensity of his heart pounding or the urgency he wished to infuse in his team of horses.

He'd danced and flirted, albeit weakly, with any number of women since meeting Lady Eva, but none provided any additional sparks of interest on his part. None filled him with longing to see them again, not like the intensity of his hope to see Lady Eva. Could he explain his feelings? Not in the slightest. Could he understand the mystery around this journey to see her again? Not any more than his feelings. And yet, here he was, journeying through the later hours of the afternoon, hoping to view the moment the full moon made its appearance.

He would have departed sooner, but his mother, unaccountably suspicious of his activities, delayed him with any number of requests. Then the roads were unseasonably wet. And his coachman insisted on more stops than usual for the horses. Oliver suspected him to be in cahoots with his mother. But at last, they had almost arrived, and he found himself fidgeting.

His mother's voice in his head harped, "Earls do not fidget." And hence he'd not fidgeted since he was but a strapping lad. Yet here he was, looking desperately for an outlet for his pent-up energy.

The sky seemed to open up, pouring all of its moisture upon them all at once. He heard the coachmen. "Easy girls." The carriage dipped and wobbled for a moment, then continued onward. The sun was a warm glow in the sky, shooting in streams of purple and orange and yellow up ahead, but here, only dark clouds filled the sky above, blocking out the early evening stars. What an interesting juxtaposition. But he was grateful because it gave them light to see.

He peeked outside the carriage window the barest amount, wondering if the rain continued on to Twickenham, when he saw two figures huddling at the side of the road.

"Stop the carriage!"

He tapped on the roof at the same time his good driver shouted, "Whoa."

They stopped and he jumped outside. The women looked wet through and freezing cold, dressed in finery. He waved to them and hurried to their side.

"Lady Anna! Upon my word." He hadn't seen the duke's dear friend in years, thought she'd moved to America or the like. "And Lady Eva!" His steps nearly froze to the mud at their feet. She'd come. And she was here, standing at the side of the road. "Oh, please, come inside." He moved quickly, his hand behind them, guiding them up and into his carriage. When they were all situated, his driver continued.

He pulled out blankets from under his seat and enjoyed the wide grateful expressions he received in response. The moment felt important, heavy with possibilities. But he found himself without many words. "You've come." He smiled.

She nodded, exchanging glances with Lady Anna.

"Lady Anna. It is delightful to see you again. The duke and his wife will be most pleased. I have reason to believe them to be attending this party as well."

"Th-thank you, my lord." Her words came out stilted, but she was likely cold.

He watched them, still uncertain Lady Eva was not an apparition. Then he realized his duties. "And where can I take you? Surely not to the ball?"

Anna frowned. "I'm afraid you are correct. Perhaps we will return to my, er, the estate, and talk things through?" She seemed to settle in more comfortably, but Lady Eva had yet to speak a word.

"We were on our way to Twickenham, decided to walk, but it took us longer than I remembered and then the rain... Thank you for coming to our aid."

He nodded. "My pleasure, as you are the very two I had hoped to see at Twickenham, my purpose in coming has been met." He tried to meet Lady Eva's gaze, but her eyes found the fabric on her blanket most interesting, apparently.

They approached the estate as the sun finally dipped below the horizon. The deluge had let up to a slow drizzle but still plenty of moisture to douse a person fell from the sky. As they gathered their things and were about to leave the blankets on his bench, he reached out in a moment of desperation. "Allow me to escort you in?"

"Certainly." Lady Anna nodded.

"And please, use these blankets as cover."

A footman came forward with an umbrella. The ladies stepped out under the cover and another man waited for Oliver. He nodded and they rushed into the house.

The women hurried up the stairs, leaving Oliver alone and feeling a bit forlorn until a cheery woman with bright eyes approached. "You are Lord Hereford?"

He dipped his head. "I am."

"I'm Mrs. Hartworth, the housekeeper. May I offer you a place by the fire and a warm cup of tea and perhaps some soup?"

"Oh that would be most appreciated. Thank you."

"Wonderful. If you would follow me, please, my lord?"

She led him away from the entryway into a front room off the side. It was decorated simply, but clean and in good repair. She pointed to the armchairs next to a roaring blaze. "That should do nicely, I would think."

"Oh yes, perfect."

"Lady Anna did say she and the Lady Eva will be down shortly."

Hope flared in his heart. "Even more excellent."

She smiled and her expression warmed him further. Then she curtseyed and left the room.

Soon he was sipping soup, eating bread and cheeses and waiting in the most pleasing fashion for Lady Eva. But there had been no happy surprise in her expression. Perhaps all the energy between them had been imagined or only felt in his own heart? He didn't know, but he wanted to stay until he found out.

EVA WAS TRYING REALLY HARD NOT TO FREAK OUT. HER breathing kept picking up to almost hyperventilation and her heart pounded one minute and then slowed to a flutter another. "What is wrong with me?"

"I don't know. Usually Aunt Nellie's tea does the trick. But you are panicking."

"Y-Yes. I guess I am. I don't mean to be." She shook. "But I'm also freezing, and from what I remember, this place has no hot running water."

Anna shook her head. "I can't believe I followed you here, without a single Advil or tampon or even a bar of soap."

"You can bring stuff when you come?" She began patting her person, looking for the journal. And then sighed in relief as she pulled it out of an inner hidden pocket, one of the features she most appreciated in her costume.

"Yes." Her eyes flickered to Eva's. "I guess that might have been helpful information."

"Uh, yeah. Like right now I could use one of my mom's Valiums."

"Not a good idea. You have your man right downstairs. We've got to get you feeling better and looking spectacular. In a Regency dress."

That made Eva laugh, and for that, she was grateful. It warmed her a bit more and relaxed some of the tension. "Too bad I don't have that hot little number you wore the other night."

"The blue sequin? Uh, yeah, no. Our duke would run, probably thinking you're trying to entrap him and the whole ton would be in a scandal."

"Wow, that bad?"

She nodded. "You need to remember the rules of Regency propriety at all times while you are here. They govern everything. Manners make or break a person in this world. And they determine people's impression. If you are well mannered, you are considered moral."

"That's ridiculous."

"In a way, to us it's ridiculous, but to them it means good breeding and therefore, well taught and well behaved."

"I guess I can see that. I'll try. I might need a refresher course."

"I'll be at your side." She pressed fingers into her temple. "I can't believe I'm here. I hope you are feeling the love, girl. It's been years since I time jumped."

"Time jumped?"

"That's just what I call it. Also, like Aunt Nellie said, if you ever get panicked—even more than now—remember it's just one month and you can go back home." She spread out her arms. "And this is the Lichfield Estate. You will always be welcome here. Even if you just want to spend your month reading."

Eva nodded, already immeasurably comforted by the thought. Two maids arrived and helped the women rid themselves of soaking wet clothing.

Once Eva was dry and was wearing several layers of clothing, plus stays and a brightly colored Regency dress, she started to feel better—all the fabric and the warmth it provided was suddenly comforting. She sat at the dressing table while the maid worked wonders on her hair in only a few moments. And the finished product was quite charming. Even with no makeup, Eva was pleased. She smiled at the young girl. "Thank you. I'd love to take you with me."

Her face turned into one of alarm. "Oh no, I couldn't leave my mum. Beggin' your pardon. Thank you for thinking of me."

Anna shook her head. "She wouldn't really take you. She just means she's pleased."

The girl curtsied. "Thank you, my lady."

As soon as both maids left, Eva whispered. "Should I be a lady? Who is my family? My father? Aren't such things known?"

"They are. But I don't know what else to do since you introduced yourself as such."

"Could I be from another country? Or America?"

"Heavens no. They're not too fond of Americans. But perhaps a northern estate in Scotland?" She shook her head. "No, just a northern English estate with an ancient family. Perhaps your father is a Baron. He doesn't serve in the house of Lords and no one has ever heard of him because he rarely leaves his estate."

"Most of that sounds like gibberish I know nothing about, but if that's the story, that's the story."

Anna reached for her hand. "And now, we go meet your new boyfriend."

"Boyfriend? That sounds so un-time period."

"I apologize. We go to...entertain the man who called."

"Better."

"Though you know this meeting is so very untoward."

Eva giggled. "I suppose it is. A man, sitting in our front room. Picked us up in the early evening in a rain storm." As she walked with Anna at her side down the stairs, she felt stronger and happier. Her heart seemed to slow and her breathing felt unrestrained. "And did you find him handsome? Or is it just my befuddled brain?"

"He's grippingly handsome." Anna fanned herself. "I highly approve. Maybe we can find one for me while we are here."

"Oh, I'd love that. The four of us could have a blast..."

Anna was shaking her head and her wry smile gave Eva pause.

"There's no double dating, no four of us, unless we're careful. Remember, we will all be chaperoned to death except in certain moments. Phaeton rides or walks are good for that. The verandah or back gardens at balls..."

"Vauxhall Gardens?"

"Yes, that's a perfect location to get lost for a time."

Eva nodded. "I understand. I'll just have to remember not to be a hoyden." She giggled again.

"And I've never heard you giggle...not one time, until today."

"I think something's still odd with me, but at least I don't feel like I need to curl up in panic."

They arrived outside the doors to the front sitting room. Anna nodded to the footman, who opened them and announced their presence.

Lord Hereford stood, placing his cup on the table to his front. "And now I am much more cheered, seeing the both of you dry and in much more pleasant circumstances."

They approached and Eva stepped forward closer. "It is in great thanks to you that we have arrived here at all." She curtseyed. "You have our deepest gratitude."

His face lit and he seemed immeasurably pleased. He bowed over her hand, and when the pressure of his lips burned through her gloves, she felt her face heat. Then he turned to Anna, doing the same. The servants brought over another chair and another tray of food and tea, and the three of them sat.

After many of the usual pleasantries, Lord Hereford directed his full attention back to Eva, and she thought she would have to hold her breath to stop it from reverting to her panicked panting. "How long will you be staying?"

"Oh, um." She looked at Anna for a hint of how to respond. "I was thinking perhaps I might have a season in London? Or half a season as it is now fully underway. I'm unsure. Thirty days at least."

"Is that because you must return here at the full moon?" His face was full of open curiosity. Eva had no idea how much he understood about the way things at Twickenham worked.

"Partly. I think it is more that Anna and I are going to return together when it's time."

"And you live in the north of England?"

"Yes, that's right."

"And your sponsor? Where might I call upon you once we all return to London?"

Eva nearly choked on her swallow of tea. She had no idea. But Anna jumped in. "My aunt, Beatrice. She's here. Or the Duke of Ramsbury. He would also be a place we stay."

"Oh well that's wonderful! The duke and duchess and I are fast friends."

"I look forward to a continued acquaintance. But before you return to London, would you like to dine with me at the inn?"

Eva rose both eyebrows. Something about his offer sounded sketchy even to her American brain.

"The both of you, of course. With a smaller party of us. The duke and his wife will be there. Tomorrow."

"Oh, yes of course. We'd love to." Eva nodded, relieved and feeling ridiculous for assuming anything different than an evening of the utmost propriety. These people governed their lives by their sense of appropriate behavior.

The rain picked up outside their window. Anna clucked. "We cannot let you go out in that. Perhaps we could settle in with a book and a quiet evening?"

"I'd like that very much."

Eva smiled. "I as well. I'm feeling a bit warm now, by the fire. Perhaps we could move to the settee?"

Lord Hereford appeared only too willing to join her at her side on the settee, and Anna took up a spot across from them in an arm chair with needlepoint in hand.

Eva looked over her shoulder at the beautiful intricate stitching. "That's lovely."

"Oh this?" She laughed, but she also seemed pleased and embarrassed. "I save it here at the house for whenever I come. Perhaps one day I will finish it."

They settled in. Lord Hereford picked up the book to his left, Shakespeare's sonnets, and began reading aloud. Eva thought she would melt from the deep timber of his voice and the lovely rhythm that washed over her. She didn't know much about how this whole adventure would move forward, but she knew one thing—she could spend many an evening in just exactly this way and be happier than she had ever been.

❦ 7 ❦

Oliver paced impatiently in the private dining room at the inn where he was staying. The duke and duchess watched him. If the expressions on their faces were any indication, both were highly amused. "You can stop laughing at me."

"Not a single jovial noise has exited my lips." The duke smirked. "Though I admit to frequent biting of my cheeks to prevent such an uncouth occurrence."

The duchess laughed at his remark, and Oliver suspected many private experiences had made it funnier than his comment merited. For Oliver found it only mildly amusing, irritating honestly, if he thought about it again. "Where are they?"

"We are here!"

He wished to have bitten his tongue right in two.

Lady Anna and Lady Eva arrived with a maid and footman. He moved forward, hands outstretched. "And so you have arrived. I'm so pleased you could come." He indicated their table. "Please join us. You remember the duke, his grace Algernon of Ramsbury, and her grace, Duchess Jane Ramsbury?"

Lady Anna nodded. "I'm so pleased to see you again, Algernon, Jane." Her eyes sparkled and she kissed both on the cheeks.

Jane squeezed her back. "I didn't think we'd be seeing you in our part of the world ever again."

Anna shrugged and indicated Eva. "When I saw her leap, without so much as an inkling of understanding, I couldn't let her come alone."

"Leap?" Oliver looked from one to the other, confused but pleased.

Also happy that Lady Anna was such a dear friend to the duke and his wife and completely lost in their conversation.

"Oh dear. I'm sorry. We are talking of our games as youth, and I apologize that no one else at the table could possibly enjoy the conversation." She took her seat. "But I do have to repeat how very good it is to see you both."

They smiled, and the duke took his wife's hand.

Then they turned to Lady Eva. "And we are so pleased to meet this new adventurous soul."

She curtseyed. "Thank you. I'm happy to be here. Though we had a rough arrival."

"Rough?"

Oliver felt at last he could contribute. "Yes, quite. I found them shivering on the side of the road. But once warm and comfortable I feel we had a lovely evening by the fire to wait out the rain." He could have thanked the rain profusely were such a thing possible. He'd never had a finer night.

"What a perfect time to arrive." The duchess shook her head.

"I couldn't have timed it better myself." The duke snorted into his cup and turned away.

Oliver began to lose a tiny bit of patience with his guests, elevated in status though they were. "Shall we begin?" He motioned for the footmen to start filling plates and cups. Conversation continued around them, but Oliver found his eyes seeking Lady Eva so much he gave up trying to resist. She didn't seem to mind and sought his thoughts as often as he sought hers. When the duke would make a joke and everyone laughed, he wanted to see the widening of her smile, how her eyes twinkled when she found something funny. And he was gratified she looked to him in those moments as well. It seemed everything merited the sharing of gazes.

By the end of the meal, he wasn't sure he could eat another meal without her sitting at his side. What a perfectly odd feeling, to have a sudden need for someone he had previously not even known existed.

"I admit to finding my arrival a bit jarring but made all the more wonderful by Lord Hereford's arrival. He was quite heroic and our evening one of the coziest and most pleasant of my life."

Oliver leaned closer to her. "I share your sentiments. Would we could bring down many more rain storms to repeat just such an evening."

The duke cleared his throat. "Perhaps we can invite you all to a dinner party at our townhome in London this Tuesday? A good introduction for Lady Eva into society?"

"Oh, thank you. I would appreciate that very much."

"And you both must stay at our home." The duchess nodded. "We have plenty of room and would love the company."

Lady Anna smiled. "I would love nothing more, as I suspect you have acquired a few more amenities?"

Everyone at the table glanced in Oliver's direction, and he'd never felt more left out of a conversation. He stood. "Perhaps a turn about the room?" He offered his arm to lady Eva.

"Oh, of course. I'd enjoy that." She stood and when she placed her hand on his arm, he felt he'd never like her to take it away. A feeling of protective energy coursed through him and he stood taller.

"I confess to seeking a moment just such as this, a tiny conversation without so many people listening."

"Oh?" Her cheeks turned a lovely pink.

"Just so." They walked slowly, for the room was not overly large. Until Oliver rested his other hand over top hers. "Would you be amenable to me calling on you?"

Eva tuned to face him. "Yes! That would be wonderful. I might be so bored if you didn't." She cleared her throat. "That would be lovely, yes."

He found her reaction so refreshing. He could tell she was well mannered and carried herself with the utmost decorum, but there was a fire, a happiness, an energy that burst forth from her that he found irresistible. "Excellent. I look forward to many moments in just such a manner as we are now and such as we had last evening by the fire. As well as walks in the park, the opera and didn't you mention Vauxhall?"

Her face lit. "You remembered."

"Naturally. We must pay a visit to the place you've most wanted to see, and to any other place you'd like to visit while in London."

They made their way back the other direction toward the other guests. As they neared, he slowed their steps once again. "My mind forbids me speak too soon, but my heart is commanding otherwise. I'll allow the two a battle and say only this much. I have never been so moved by a woman." He bowed over her hand, pressing his lips once again on her knuckles.

When they returned to the table, something had changed between them, a new sort of understanding felt comfortable and unsettling all at once. Oliver wasn't sure he'd ever sleep well again with thoughts of Lady Eva running through his mind. But as he watched her laugh with the others and eat and feel more comfortable, he imagined more and more what life might be like with her at his side, and he couldn't imagine a happier way to be.

❧ 8 ❧

Eva paced her small room, the lady's maid waiting patiently for her to begin dressing. Anna sat in a chair over by the fair, already dressed and ready.

"But he has expectations." Eva wrung her hands together.

"They will all have hopes. Will want to dance with you, call on you, fill up your afternoons. But their hopes do not require anything from you. You behave according to your own desires."

Eva groaned. "But how could I pursue anything more than a mild flirtation with anyone, knowing that I will be gone within the month?"

"But will you? Be gone? You don't know that. Anything could happen. Remember, you can return at any time to any time. Right when you left."

Eva stopped. "I keep forgetting that all important detail. When I freak out, will you please remind me?"

She nodded and then indicated the maid. "That's precisely why I am here, wearing stays, using a chamber pot again and submitting myself to mindless ballroom chatter."

"You are the dearest friend."

"I know. Now, let's get you beautified."

Eva held up her arms and the maid pulled off her nightshift, quickly replacing it with all her various underthings. When at last the emerald green gown flowed over her head and down to the floor, she felt strapped in and drowning in clothing. But as she stepped in front of her mirror, even she had to admit the effect was stunning. "Remarkable."

Anna nodded. "You will awe and amaze."

"As will you. Have you thought what you will do if some Earl comes calling your name?"

"Well, if he's anything like yours, I might be convinced to stay awhile." She smiled and Eva sat down at her dressing table. The maid used a new pomade on her cheeks, which brought out some natural looking color. And then the Regency version of a curling iron, which probably fried the ends to smithereens, produced lovely ringlets of hair around Eva's face. The maid hid jewels throughout her hair so that it would sparkle in the candlelight, then applied a touch of rose water to her neck.

"If I might say so, you look lovely." Her maid curtseyed and bowed her head.

"Oh, thank you. You've turned me into a royal princess. You're a wonder."

"I'm happy to have pleased you. If that will be all?"

"Yes, I'll return and ring for you before bed."

"Very good, my lady."

As soon as the maid was out of the room, Eva eyed herself again. "It really is remarkable what they can accomplish without a lick of mascara or foundation."

"Two other products I wish I'd brought with us."

"So, you know to let the servants put food on your plate?"

"Yes, and fill my cup. I know not to eat until the host eats. I am to stick to boring subjects."

"But to try to make them sound decidedly not boring."

"I love how you all of a sudden use words like 'decidedly.'"

"I told you I've lived here for months at a time. It would do you well to try to adopt a certain manner of speaking. At least you can pull off the British sounding vowels."

"And if they ask about my manner of speaking?"

"Hopefully our story of you being isolated your whole life will aid in the believability of you being English." She laughed. "And from their time period."

"This is the greatest immersion of all time. I still can't believe we pulled this off."

"It's incredible to know such an opportunity exists. I'm not sure how the Fae choose people to bless with this knowledge, but it's priceless."

Eva considered. "I could go any time I wanted."

"You could. I think Nellie is much more inclined to help in matters of the heart, but she's been known to support a bit of healthy curiosity and adventure as well."

Eva smiled. "Shall we?"

"Yes, I'm certain the guests will soon be arriving, and I'm dying to talk to Jane."

"She sounds kind of...modern."

"I'll let her tell you her story."

Eva nodded and then she smiled. "I can't believe I've got my own Earl coming to dine at a Regency dinner party."

"Let's see who else Jane invited for me to meet."

Eva laughed. "And off we go." She corrected. "What I meant to say was, let us not be late to greet the guests."

"Better."

They descended just as the butler let in the first of the guests. Two men, not as broad shouldered as Lord Hereford, but dashing in their cravats in the breadth their jackets stretched across their shoulders. They laughed and joked with the duke and he introduced her and Anna to his friends.

"Lady Eva, Miss Anna, these are some of my closest friends from childhood. Doesn't mean I recommend them as honorable, but they are good hearted."

"Our best friend is mis-representing us to you lovely ladies." The one called Lord Castlebury bowed. "I am pleased to meet you both and would be honored if you would sit beside me."

"They can't both sit by you because at least one is invited to sit by me." The man at his side bowed next to his friend. "And I am Lord Tillsdale." He stood taller. "And we have known Algernon his whole life. Jane's the best thing ever to happen to that man, but likewise couldn't have happened to a better woman. We're happy for them both."

Eva smiled. She liked these two and could tell they were all about the fun, maybe the partiers from her day, the guys up for a one night stand. She wondered how that worked during Regency. Did they just flirt with abandon? She determined to watch carefully. "I'm happy to meet you. Anna and I arrived yesterday."

"Perhaps we could show you around London, go on a ride through the park?"

"After she rides with me." Lord Hereford approached and towered over everyone in the room. She knew he was large in stature, but she had no idea just how large. Especially by English standards and genetics of this time, he looked like a giant.

Her grin grew. "Lord Hereford. How good to see you."

The men looked from her to him and back, then seemed to fade away into the background, and Anna drifted off with them. Eva thought that amusing. Lord Hereford reached for her hand to place on his arm. "I'm happy to see you as well." His gaze drifted over to the men who were making Anna laugh. "I see you've met some of my set."

"Yes, they're lively, fun."

"Good words for them. Men with good hearts."

"That's what the duke said, too."

"Then I stand by my confirmation of the truth. Finer men you might never meet. Once they settle down they might even make good husbands."

Eva laughed. "And what about you? If they're your friends does that mean people say the same of you?"

He looked troubled for a moment, and Eva's interest heightened.

"What would people say of me? The answer to that question might be quite valuable if one were to know it." He looked thoughtful. "I'd imagine certain ladies might say the same of me." He wiggled his eyebrow. "But those are the ladies of a set who don't know me very well."

"So you might be open to the opportunity for a little fun, even entertainment of a more reckless nature?" She knew her eyes flashed challenge. She was curious what he would say.

But he answered, not missing a single beat. "I've never heard a more delightful proposition from a woman."

"What? Is Lady Eva already propositioning you?" The duke suddenly stood beside them and spoke in undertones.

"Absolutely not." Eva was dismayed at his insinuation.

"Algernon, behave." Lord Hereford joked. "We are in the presence of one I would hope to impress."

"Very well. I thought I'd heard something scandalous. I must have misheard."

He stepped away obviously highly amused with himself.

"I apologize for my friend. For all my friends."

"No need at all. I am pleased to hear you have a sense of adventure and a desire to enjoy some of the sights of England?"

"With you, anything will be a delight. I find your openness refreshing, engaging." He nudged closer. "And alluring." His lovely cologne washed over her in a tantalizing smell as he dipped closer to her. Had he said alluring? Mmm. His very closeness drew her in like nothing she'd even known.

"Thank you."

The duke called them into dinner. He led his wife in first. Then Lord Hereford held his arm out to Eva and he went in second. Second. He was second in nobility to the duke! She wondered his story and determined to learn his family tree. Anna followed on the arm of one of the duke's friends, Lord Castlebury. Two by two, they all entered.

The table was dressed in such an appealing manner that Eva sucked in her breath. "Why. This is lovely."

Jane turned to her and smiled. "I do enjoy thinking up some of this myself, so I thank you."

Each place had a name card. Lord Hereford led her around the table until they found their names, thankfully situated together. He held out her chair and she sat, along with the other women in the room. Then when they were all seated, the duchess nodded and the duke called for the meal to begin.

Eva had never been so enchanted. At a nod from Jane, attractive men in well-fitting uniforms placed just the right amount of food on her plate and within moments, everyone had their first course. The duke picked up his spoon and they all took their first bite of soup.

"Mm. Oh your grace, this is delicious." Eva called to Jane at the other end of the table.

Everyone stopped eating to stare at her. She looked to Anna who only appeared amused but shook her head a tiny bit. What had she done wrong?

The more they ate, the more bored Eva became. Lord Hereford talked of the weather three times. Then he mentioned an upcoming ball. He asked about her hobbies, her "proficiencies" he called them. And she could only guess what would be appropriate to answer. She thought back to *Pride and Prejudice* and the many immersive events she'd participated in. Anna's needlepoint came to mind. "I enjoy needlepoint. I love to draw."

He nodded, a glazed look overtaking his face.

She obviously failed at making boring conversation exciting. And Lord Hereford didn't look any more willing to give it a go than she. She looked up and down the table for a moment. In only a month, she was leaving, no matter what happened. There was nothing she could say to damage the duke and duchess—they were a ducal couple. "Well, I for one would like to know why they haven't allowed the waltz at Almack's." Was that scandalous enough?

The men rolled their eyes. And Lord Tillsdale snorted. "Because it's Almacks."

The duchess grinned. "I heard it from the most reputable source that they are beginning to allow it, but that each person has to gain individual approval before you are allowed to dance it."

The women in the room looked significantly more excited than the men. But Eva found the conversation interesting. So, talking about the waltz was not scandalous. At least it created something unique to say. The ladies started talking about when they'd learned to waltz.

Lord Hereford smiled. "We've had the waltz at most grand balls besides Almacks this season, and no one has been scandalized."

The duchess laughed. "Almost no one."

"True. A few of the more conservative among us might have fainted straight away, the first time the three-step music started."

Eva laughed. "And what about Prinny? Hasn't he been dancing the waltz for years?"

"Oh, well of course. But his wife's from Germany. It came to his household through her, he says."

"Right, but we all know he doesn't even talk to the woman, let alone dance with her."

"But if you are so unfortunate as to be invited to a party at Prinny's, you expect a certain lack of propriety and are expected to keep it to yourself."

"Ah, what happens at Prinny's, stays at Prinny's. Is that it?"

The men at the table burst into laughter. The duke and duchess most especially burst into fits, and Anna snorted into her lemonade.

"My, but she's clever." Lord Tillsdale looked her over in such an appraising appreciation that Lord Hereford bristled beside her, and she looked away, embarrassed.

The duke raised his cup. "To a new phrase that will soon spread throughout the ton." He winked at her. "Coined by our clever Lady Eva."

They raised their cups in salute and everyone took a sip.

The second and third courses came and went, and Eva felt like she wouldn't be able to take another bite. But the conversation had picked up, and she was happy for a slightly braver group. "I have another thing I'd like to understand better."

Everyone eyed her, Anna looking slightly nervous on her behalf, but Lord Hereford's expression of expectation made her grin. "I want to understand this whole idea of a blue stocking. Men, do you really wish for your wife not to be educated on certain subjects?"

"Ooh, I'd be careful how I answered that one." The duchess laughed. "That's a trap if I ever saw one."

Eva dipped her head. "True enough. But it's something I've given years of thought, and I'd love a first-hand response."

The men looked slightly uncomfortable, but Lord Hereford tapped his fingers on the tabletop. "Might I have a go?"

She held out her hands. "By all means."

"I have been considering this very topic quite often in the past month already, without you asking. And I've been paying attention to our topics of conversation and the ladies who are all quite lovely, but limited in the subjects about which they converse. I think we might do ourselves a disservice to reject the more forward thinking of our women, or to steer clear of one who wants to study the more advanced subjects."

Eva nodded. His response was a decent beginning to a well thought out and fair understanding. She was impressed. "And those who wish to talk of politics, who would enjoy groups that study the arts and the latest poets. Perhaps even Byron could join such a group to share his latest words. What think you of these?"

Lord Hereford nodded. "Again, I'd welcome the change." He looked around the table at the guests, who had the varying degrees of discomfort. "I don't say I speak for everyone here."

The duchess smiled. "You've asked a question at a friendly table. For I hold discussions like those you speak of weekly here in my home. You're welcome to join us this Thursday."

"Oh, I'd be most interested."

"And I." Lord Hereford glanced back at Eva for approval, which she heartily gave.

The duchess raised her eyebrow. "I'd be interested to hear what you make of our talks, Lord Hereford."

"And I'd be honored to attend."

"This very week we are welcoming two of the most forward thinkers of our time."

The silence that responded to her statement told Eva a few things about how the ton viewed her guests.

"But the dukes of Northumberland and Cumberland will also be present, and I do believe we've convinced Sussex to join us."

"Royal Dukes? Excellent!"

"If he can find it in himself to travel. But he has agreed to come and finds news of our discussions most intriguing."

The conversation continued until the men separated and the women were left to themselves for a moment. Anna approached and under her breath, Eva mumbled. "Does no one talk in this century?"

"They talk. They're just selective about what they say."

Eva hoped that perhaps she could continue nudging the conversation into interesting subjects. Either way, her efforts seemed to attract Lord Hereford. She just needed to decide if that was a good thing.

❧ 9 ❧

Oliver found himself thinking of Lady Eva quite a bit more than he thought about anyone or anything else. At breakfast he wondered how she preferred her eggs. Then as he sat to answer correspondence, he wondered at her hand in writing letters, and that led him to wonder if he would ever receive a letter from her own hand. Then he realized that such a thing would mean they were engaged to be married and he shocked himself at his great delight in such a thought.

After walking the back length of his home for over a quarter an hour, puzzling over why the woman could have such a hold on him, his mother shooed him out of the house. "We have this lovely park. Go be in it." She waved her hand.

His pace picked up in a rapid effort to lose some of his energy and distract himself from Lady Eva's smile, which was at present the only thing he could think of for any great length of time. All other thoughts flitted about and left the moment they entered his awareness. He shook his head. It was still incredibly early to be out wandering the park, and he was grateful—for it meant he wasn't likely to meet a single other person as he tried to sort through his feelings.

Hadn't he just been hoping to meet someone like Lady Eva, someone he could perhaps grow into a love match? But his feelings had escalated so quickly, and that made him uncomfortable. He didn't know her. No one had heard of her family. And his mother would certainly have opinions about her. But Eva was so refreshingly bold, so real.

He laced his fingers behind his back and paced in front of a large water fountain. The mist from the falling water drifted and bounced through the air in tiny droplets, refreshing his upturned face. What was he concerned about, really? He could simply get to know the woman. He was in perfect control of his actions, was he not? Emotion, attraction or not, he could move forward with a rational approach as well as anyone.

"Lord Hereford?" Her voice shook him to his core, and he stopped himself from gripping his chest, but only barely. *Lady Eva*. She approached from a nearby copse of trees, her hair falling freely around her shoulders, wearing what might be a morning dress? But it looked as though she'd casually thrown it on. She adjusted one shoulder so that it did not slide down again, baring her skin.

He swallowed twice before speech would come. "Lady Eva." He clipped his heels together and bowed. He stepped closer, drawn with a power he hardly knew how to counter. "It's good to see you this morning."

She smiled and her whole face lit. "And you as well. I was thinking how such a lovely walk would be benefited by excellent company."

He held out his arm for her to take. "And do I qualify as such company for you?"

She paused a moment until he turned his gaze back to her face. "You are the most excellent."

His heart pounded in response. Unsure what to say, he dipped his head. "Those words from you have twice their value."

She smiled as though she guarded a well-kept secret.

"Might I ask your thoughts?"

"You may." She skipped a step, still holding fast to his arm. "I was thinking how well-spoken you are and how delightful it is to hear such things with a well-turned phrase."

He found that curious, especially as he was unable to put two words together very well at the moment, but if his manner pleased her, all the better.

He looked over her shoulder. "Let's not lose your maid…" He searched in vain for anyone following. Then he turned, aghast. "Have you come alone?"

To his great surprise, her face colored with guilt. "I didn't wish to wake her."

"Wake her? She was undoubtedly awake…"

"Oh, was she? I guess I didn't think of it." Her gaze dropped and her slipper nudged a rock at her feet out in front of her gown. "I sought some solitude this morning. No one knows I slipped away."

He shook his head, uncertain how to proceed. They were alone without chaperone, her without even so much as a maid. "I should deliver you to the duke's home."

"Must you? So soon?" Her eyes widened and he was almost overcome with happiness at the evidence she wished to be with him.

"Well. It would be the gentlemanly thing to do. It would never do to be caught alone here in the park. And since you didn't inform anyone, they will undoubtedly be concerned."

"If we must return, then we must. But perhaps a quick turn before? No one will be up for hours yet."

He hesitated, then nodded. "I would be pleased to take a turn. And then equally pleased to return you to your friends."

"Thank you."

They turned down a lesser used path. "I've walked these paths since I was a young lad."

"Have you? Which is your favorite?"

He shook his head, grinning.

"What? Have I said something inappropriate?"

"No, not at all, on the contrary. I find myself continually delighted by the things that come out of your mouth. No one has ever asked me such a question, not even my mother." He frowned. "And now I must think of a suitable response." He picked up their pace. "If we hurry, we can make it there before you must return."

"Oh, how exciting." She seemed genuinely interested which again he found refreshing.

In not more than a few moments, he turned into a path lined with hedgerows. "This is my favorite." The hedges rose up to their waists. "When I was young, it was quite a challenging maze for me to navigate." He winked.

"And for others to come find you."

"Precisely. I could lengthen out our walks in the park by another hour at least because of this path."

"I see the cleverness of it."

"Now you tell me something you enjoyed from childhood."

"Ah, let me see. You might appreciate this one. I used to spend time dreaming up all the things I'd love to do if I ever had a season in London."

"Did you, now!"

"I did. And I made a list, in a journal I have. I call it a bucket list."

"A bucket list?"

"Yes, you know, things to fill up my bucket with before I die."

"Interesting. I've never heard it called that. But tell me. What are some more of the things on this list of yours?"

"You'll think me so randomly silly I don't know if I dare."

"How can I be a part of your wish fulfillment if you don't tell me?"

She lifted her lashes, and the expression she gifted him was so full of appreciation he almost pulled her into his arms right then.

"I wish to see a perfumaria. And another merchant to buy ribbons."

"So far your requests seem so perfectly mundane, I confess to being quite disappointed."

"How ungallant."

"Surprise me. Show me you are as I suspect—delightfully unique, a step above the other women I know."

"If you think you can handle my outlandish thoughts."

"Handle?"

"Oh, um, if you think you will still be interested..."

"I have no doubt of that."

"I'd like to dance near the banks of the Thames with the moonlight shining on the water."

He nodded.

"I'd like to see the Elgin Marbles."

He coughed.

"I'd like to visit a museum."

Easy enough, that one.

"The opera, a poetry reading. A musicale. Oh, and I must *must* be present when Beau Brummel gets his cravat tied."

"How do you plan to manage that feat?"

"Perhaps he will take to doing public demonstrations." She shrugged like she knew something, and Oliver would not have been the least surprised if she did.

"I'd like to see Prinny, but not meet him. But I would love to meet the Duke of Wellington."

A touch of jealousy tugged at his peace of mind. "You would?"

"Certainly. Wouldn't you? Oh and Blake Shelley and also Lord Byron." She held a hand to her heart. For a moment he thought her quite near fainting.

"This is probably not at all likely, given the distance. But I had not even considered how wonderful it would be to meet a woman by the name of Jane Austen."

He frowned, trying to place her.

"She wrote the book, *Pride and Prejudice*."

"I haven't had the privilege of reading such a book. So, this woman is an author, you say?"

"Yes, one of the most talented of my day."

"Your day?"

"That is to say, those who have read her book are enchanted. We anxiously await her next."

He committed the information to memory. If he ever came across such a book, he would know what to do with it.

"And now, tell me something you find most difficult."

"I cannot abide disappointing others. Now you."

"I find it difficult to relax in large groups."

"Do you? As do I. I much prefer the private more intimate conversations." She stepped closer almost without thinking.

"And so do I." He lifted her hand in his own. "But most especially with you." He pressed his lips to her bare hand, the velvety softness sending ripples of expectation up her arm.

"Oh."

He turned her hand over and then pressed his lips to her wrist. "While we are yet alone, I must tell you, I have longed to do just this." He pressed his lips to her wrist again, lingering longer. "And this." He kissed her again, slightly higher.

She was astounded at what a kiss could do to a person. She reached out her other hand to steady herself on his arm.

"I want very much to have many more moments such as these."

She lifted her chin to wonder at his sincerity, and all she saw was an intensity that drew her closer.

"I as well." Her dress slipped down off her shoulder.

His eyes travelled along the bareness of her skin exposed and then up to her face.

Everywhere he looked sent waves of awareness. His gaze moved to her lips and they moved together, closer, her head giddy with a spinning desire. Her mouth parted. And then he backed away. "Forgive me. I quite forget myself."

She adjusted her dress and ran hands down the front of her skirts. "Me, too. I think."

After a moment of awkwardness, he lifted his time piece up out of his pocket. "We must return. Good heavens, the time has passed rather quickly."

He led her as swiftly as he could without rushing unnecessarily until they stood at the duke's front step.

When the butler opened the door, to his credit he did not react but simply gave them space to enter. Oliver turned through the front room and made his way to where he knew they might have started their breakfast.

"You know your way around."

"I do. I have been the happy recipient of many an invitation here at the ducal townhome."

Jane smiled in welcome as they entered the breakfast room. "Yes, we enjoy Oliver whenever he will deign to spend some time with us."

"It is always my pleasure, you can be assured of that." He bowed. "Your grace."

"And you." Jane looked to Lady Eva with eyebrows raised. "I suppose you were outside of these walls dressed in such a state?"

Eva looked down at herself, readjusting her sleeve once again so that it rested on her shoulder. "I suppose I'm a bit disheveled."

Jane laughed, looking to Oliver. "And we have you to thank for the rescue?"

"It was my pleasure, I assure you."

"Well, you must stay for breakfast." She indicated the service on the side of the room.

"I would be delighted. Thank you."

Lady Eva and he filled their plates, and he was pleased to discover she liked her eggs just how he did.

As he sat to eat, he realized he couldn't have felt more cozy, more at home than he did in that moment. He didn't know her as well as he would like, but there was much to be said about general ease of knowing. And she had that in a great abundance.

Perhaps it was time to mention her to his mother.

❧ 10 ❧

As soon as Lord Hereford left, Jane pulled her into the duke's office and shut the door. "Okay, spill."

"Oh my gosh! You aren't gonna believe what just went down. Hold on. Did you just say, 'Okay, spill'?" She crossed her arms. "Something you want to tell me?"

"I thought you knew. Algernon and I met when he came forward to 2020."

Eva stared, not sure what to make of this woman. "I knew it! So you really are Jane Sullivan, from my time?"

"Yup."

"And you're living here forever? As a duchess?" She squealed. "That's insane and so totally awesome I don't even know what to do with that information."

"I go back now and then. It wears on you after a while, the time hops, but I need to bring back some supplies. And I grab a donut. You know, the important things."

She rubbed her temples. "I don't even know what to do with this information."

"You said that."

"True. Okay." She plopped down in an armchair. "For starters, I think you living here as a duchess is incredible. Do you know how many men you could help? How many women you could help?"

"It's not as easy as you think."

"I don't see why not. You walk up to someone, 'Hey, you don't have to put up with this, you know that right?'"

"It took two hundred years to get where we are today."

Eva waved her hands. "We can talk about that later. I gotta tell you what happened, and you've gotta help me know what to do."

She told her about the almost kiss, the great talks, the amazing energy between them. And then she frowned. "But I can't fall in love with this guy. I'd feel terrible if I was encouraging him to fall in love with me."

"It may be too late. Oliver has never acted like that before. I'm sure you've noticed he is the king of propriety. So if he is acting like this, I'd say he's about a hair's breadth away from proposing."

"What!" Eva choked. "We don't even know each other."

Jane shrugged. "That doesn't matter. He can probably tell you two would get on well together, and you're the best woman he's ever talked to hands down." She laughed. "It's so nice to talk like an American again."

"But I'm not like you. I came here for a month's vacation. I have no intention of living here forever. What am I gonna do?"

"That's something you will have to decide. I can't help you there. But if you do decide to figure out if Oliver is worth it, I will tell you that of all Algernon's friends, Oliver is the absolute best. And he's fun to look at."

"He's so hot. I should have kissed him."

"Well now, remember if you're caught kissing someone, they will feel obligated to propose. It will set up a whole expectation here in the ton."

"I'll just have to make sure I don't get caught." She tapped her hands together. "But he would take it to mean something more serious, wouldn't he?"

"Of course. Especially Oliver."

She nodded. What a quandary. She could not in good conscience do that to him. "Should I tell him about where or *when* I'm from?"

Jane considered her for a long moment, longer than Eva felt was necessary. "I don't know. Not yet. It's a risky thing to let too many people know about the opportunities that come with time travel. I suspect he is meant to know, because you and he are so obviously drawn to each other. But it really isn't my decision to make."

"Who's is it?"

"I think yours."

Eva thought that over. "True. Because what if I tell him and he follows me home?" The idea sounded more romantic than anything she could imagine. "Wait a minute. Isn't that what *you* did?"

"More or less. I'll have to tell you about the time I spent in New York City, dating the duke."

"This I gotta hear."

"Maybe tomorrow night. We can have an old-fashioned slumber party, and you can hear mine and Anna's stories." Eva smirked.

"Anna has a story?"

"Oh, she's got many. Most I don't even know about."

"Well, this I gotta hear."

"But in the meantime, I can't lead him on," Eva frowned. "I can't keep seeing him especially if he's thinking all of this is a fast track to marriage. I don't want to tell him about the time travel yet. But I do think we should relax and have some fun. Maybe I can scare him off with my uncouth and almost scandalous ways." The idea brought a twinge of sadness.

"I don't think you're gonna lose him that quickly."

"You underestimate my powers."

Her smile turned secretive. "No, you underestimate your power." She wrapped an arm across her shoulders. "And I happen to know he'll be here to pick you up to picnic at Vauxhall Gardens tomorrow."

"Oh, that's right." She moaned. "I suppose I'll have to start turning him away then."

"If you insist. But that doesn't sound very fun. Do you know how many women would die to have a specimen like him in their lives?"

"But at what cost? Do you never miss people back home?"

"I go visit. And yes. I miss them sometimes, but my parents were done with me. They've since moved to Italy, rented a house there."

Jane's words stung. Did Eva's own family feel that way about her? They certainly were involved in their own lives. The memory of the phone being dropped on the floor last time she called stung. Did her mother even know that Eva was in England? She snorted. She certainly didn't know she was in 18-hundred-something England, but she suspected she hadn't really paid enough attention to the call to know Eva was out of the country.

———

OLIVER STEPPED OUT OF HIS CARRIAGE AND REACHED BACK to help Jane down. His servants gathered the items for their picnic to set up in their designated spot. When his hands touched hers, even gloved, he felt the familiar happy expectation he'd come to expect.

She smiled up into his face, and he recognized a glint of something worrisome. Was it dangerous? Recklessness? It seemed to him to hold a desperate quality about it. But she behaved as she had the last time they'd been together.

"Tell me, did you bring the journal?"

She patted her overly large reticule. "I did. We can be entertained while we rest on our walk."

"Excellent." He secretly wished to know the entirety of her list. If he could fill every one of her buckets, how happy that would make him. And perhaps that would also convince her to want to be with him, for he knew that as much as he was engaged in trying to make a relationship with her, she was not so engaged. But he couldn't ascertain why. For he suspected she was as equally attracted. He'd seen her pull away, seen the regret and the hesitation to do so. Still, he would persist. He had all the time he could need and plenty of patience.

They walked through the entrance. "There are quite a few people out here today, aren't there?" She looked around with wide eyes, and he was gratified again that he was gifting her with something she'd wanted to do for so long.

"They're here for the surprise."

"Oh? What surprise?"

He pointed to a large colorful fabric on the ground, attached to many ropes.

"Is that?"

"A balloon."

"What? Like a hot air balloon?"

His confusion must have been obvious because she said, "Meaning, it flies on the hot air?"

"Yes, you are correct, but I've never heard it called thus, and it is a relatively new custom. How is it you've heard of such a thing?"

"Oh, um." She looked away. "It might be new here, but in our small part of the world, hot air balloons, as we call them, are a huge part of our local parties."

Disappointment filled him. "Oh, so I won't be adding anything new to your list then."

"Oh, now, everything about you is adding new things to my list. Never worry about that. If you are anything, you are new."

He wasn't sure what to think about that answer. They walked through the long archway covered by trees creating a canopy above their heads. A light breeze cooled them, and Oliver didn't think he could have made the day any more perfect. But he puzzled over why everything about him would be so new. Perhaps because she had fewer families with which to associate where she lived.

They made their way to the back, more woodsy part of the park. He led her down the first path, knowing that it turned and weaved through the trees for quite a distance and that they would be lost from sight for as long as they desired. Perhaps he could enjoy her journal and hear more of her plans. And he might share a few of his own.

The path grew immediately more shady and Lady Eva sighed. "This is lovely. What a beautiful place." She looked up at him. "Where does the park touch the banks of the river? Do people really arrive by boat?"

"They do, and that's part of the other surprise. We will be departing in that manner to return you to your home."

"What! Really!" She clapped her hands and jumped a little bit, in much the same manner as he remembered doing as a child.

Perhaps part of her charm was that no one had stifled the human exuberance out of her. He would never tire of the study of Lady Eva.

Their path opened up to a small circular garden area with a fountain in the center. "Oh this is charming as well."

They walked the edge of the circle and then approached a bench. Oliver dipped his head. "Shall we?"

She nestled down, and he sat beside her. As close as he dared. "Let's see this journal, then."

"We can check one off."

"Check it off?"

"Yes, we make a mark next to the list item, and it means we accomplished it."

"I understand what you mean by marking it finished. I was wondering what we are checking off?"

"This visit to Vauxhall of course. Remember?"

"Oh yes. How do you hope to cross it off?" He leaned over her shoulder.

She opened her mouth, then closed it. Then she smiled and shook her head. "Ah, because we've no ink or quill." She waved her hand. "I'll do it later." She opened the first few pages, skimmed past much writing he'd love to read some day, and then stopped on a well-worn page.

"Here we go. Keep in mind, I've been working on this list for a long time, so some of the items might seem young. Or unimportant." The slight pink of her cheeks was quite charming, and he hoped to bring it back to her lovely expression again in the future.

He scanned the written page as quickly as he could and he saw the typical items he would expect, some of which she had already shared with him: the opera, the museum, a perfumaria, Ackermans—he chuckled at that one—the horse races. "Horse races? How can you possibly hope to see those? Or Jacksons? Whites?"

She snatched it back. "If you're going to have opinions about my list, I can keep it to myself."

He laughed. "No, please, show me. I won't say another word except in undying support."

She held the book up to her chest for a couple heartbeats then leaned forward again, their arms pressed together, and he felt the situation the happiest circumstance. "See here. I want to see the theater as well. I'd love to dance once at Almacks." Her brow lifted wickedly. "The waltz."

"Ho ho! Why am I not even surprised?"

His eyes followed her finger to another item on the list. "And what's this?"

"Oh, right, that. So—"

"Touch the hem of Lady Jersey's gown? Borrow an item from her person?"

She pulled the book back away from him. "This section is probably off limits. It's about experiences." She glanced down again. "Oh, yes, totally off limits." She pressed the opened book to her chest.

He tried his most endearing, pleading expression which felt deliciously new to him.

Her smile grew and she succumbed. "I can tell you a couple." She held up a finger. "But certainly not all, so do not ask. Watch Beau Brummel tie a cravat you've seen. I'd like to see Prinny. Ride a phaeton through Hyde Park. Become hopelessly lost with a gentleman in a hedge maze."

"Did our maze count?"

She pressed her lips together, pretending to ponder his question which he found irresistible, unaccountably. The expression had never had a similar effect from other women.

"Were we 'hopelessly' lost?"

"No, but that hardly signifies. There's not a maze in England in which we would become hopelessly lost. All you have to do is walk the perimeter—"

She held up her hand. "You are ruining the magic."

He pressed his lips together.

She checked her book again and then laid it back in her lap. "And those are enough experiences for one lifetime, I would think."

He knew she was hiding something he was desperate to know. But he'd just have to be happy with what they'd discussed so far. He pulled out his watch fob. "If we head back now, there is an event I know you'll be happy to see."

"Oooh, what is it?"

"A surprise makes it even better."

"True. Let's go see this exciting surprise." She jumped to her feet.

He rose next to her, the curls of her hair tickling his chin. Before he stepped away, he breathed in her lovely scent. She even smelled differently than most women. A clean, freshness hovered about her, and he was filled with a surprising desire to press his face into her curls, inhaling deeply.

As if sensing his charged emotion, she looked up, her blue eyes stark against the creamy softness of her skin, the space between them shrinking with each breath. Her nose was delightfully pert and tipped up on the end, her lips close, so close he felt a puff of her breath on his chin. And he was frozen with desire.

The world around them slowed and became silent. Nothing but the pounding of blood through his veins and the tiniest puffs of breath on his skin mattered. Then her mouth parted and she wet her lips. Her swallow enchanted him. Without thinking, he lifted a hand and wrapped one of her curls around his finger, gently toying with the softness of her hair. He leaned forward and pressed his lips to her forehead.

So much more he wanted with this woman who earned such a hold on his heart. But he kept himself in check. Patience, hope, a gentle and slow courtship would someday win her heart.

When he stepped back, her eyes filled with that same hope and a flash of disappointment. Had she wished to be kissed, soundly and thoroughly? Because he had certainly wished to oblige. He could wait. When they were properly and appropriately engaged, if she were to ever grant that happiest of unions, then he might attempt such a thing.

❧ 11 ❧

L ord Hereford led her out of the walking paths through the woods, back through the mini sized maze and down the other direction of the gardens, towards the large crowd and the huge colorful fabric. She sucked in her breath. "Oh, this is incredible. I had no idea they did these back then!"

"Pardon?" Lord Hereford's frown of confusion jolted her back to remembering that he was not from her time, did not know anything about time travel and she needed to never ever forget that. In fact, now would be an excellent time to start trying to push him away. But as she looked into his adorably confused and hopeful eyes, she couldn't bring herself to do anything that would change his appreciative gaze. At least not today. Tomorrow. She would start to try pushing him away tomorrow.

The hot air balloon towered above them in bright yellows and greens. Many ropes tied it to the ground on each side. A group of people stood on a platform next to a small box attached to the ropes and balloon.

"How exactly does this work?" She tipped her head.

"The gasses keep rising, pulling the balloon in the air," Lord Hereford explained. "Then everyone here races across the countryside following it until they reach the end of their ride."

"Then what happens?"

"The most exciting part. Those in that box fall."

She gasped.

"With the box, mind you. It's not as bad as all that."

She found it just as bad as all that. But she said nothing, waiting in horror for what would happen next.

"A parachute opens and carries them down to the ground safely."

She had many doubts about the whole manner in which this would carry out. "And do many get injured in such an activity?"

"Of course not. It's perfectly safe."

"Hmm." But she smiled. When would she ever get to see such a thing? Did Regency experts know that hot air balloon rides were accomplished during this time and in such a manner? "This should have been on my bucket list."

"Could you add it so that we might cross it off?"

She laughed. "You are so much like me. I was thinking that very thing."

"Then we are of one mind. We shall add it tonight and then cross it off together." He placed her hand on his arm. "As well as Vauxhall and riding in a boat from here."

"Are you going to attempt them all?"

"I can safely promise not to take you to Whites or Jacksons boxing."

"Don't ever promise anything you don't completely control."

He dipped his head back and laughed, and Eva was transfixed by the sound. Deep lovely happiness bubbled out of him in pure enjoyment and rippled through her until her very core called out to her to try to make him laugh again and again, every day for the rest of her life. She gasped. What a thought. She placed a hand over her mouth, happy that no one could hear her brain ticking, especially not Lord Hereford.

He turned to face her, standing almost as close as before, but now with people all around them. "If you keep looking at me like that, I'm going to promise not to resist my ungentlemanly thoughts."

Her mouth dropped. Had Lord Hereford just come on to her?

His eyes burned through her, tugging at her in ways she had not been expecting during their walk in the park. She stared deeply back into his eyes, forgetting where they were, forgetting everything around them. Until someone cleared their throat.

She turned slowly, her brain sluggish. So much that she had to blink twice before she recognized the duke and duchess.

Jane laughed and then latched herself onto Eva's arm while the duke took Lord Hereford away.

"What are you doing?" Eva heard the whine in her voice and didn't even care.

Jane laughed. "Oh honey. You're in the middle of the park. Come on now, let's go watch a ridiculously archaic hot air balloon ride."

"Oh! Oh yes, that's right. Have you seen one of these? Does this actually work?"

"Believe it or not, it does. I haven't seen a fatality yet."

"Should I be encouraged?"

"Absolutely. Quite a few broken bones, mind you, and much tumbling out of the basket upon landing, but no deaths."

They approached the outer edge of the crowd gathered around the balloon and the platform. Two groups of people stood near where the ropes were tethered into the ground. A man came forward, shouting out to the crowd. "Gather round."

Everyone pressed forward.

"We will commence our launch at the count of ten."

The crowd shouted. "Ten, nine, eight, seven, six, five, four, three, two..." On one, the people at the ropes tugged and pulled on them until the web roping that covered the top of the balloon fell to the ground and the people in the basket rose up into the air.

Eva stared and wished for her phone. No one in a million years would anyone ever believe she had seen such a thing. Jane watched her face and laughed. "Oh, my dear, it is so wonderful to have you here. It's even better than when Anna comes to visit. It's not new for her anymore."

Eva laughed. "Where is she?"

"She's taken to sleeping and reading and resting in our family rooms."

She had told Eva to go on without her, that she'd already seen and done everything.

"You'll come visit next time you travel forward won't you? At least call? I'll leave my number."

Jane was quiet and Eva turned to her. The woman's eyes were serious, sad almost. "Will you not even consider staying?"

Eva looked away, a peculiar sadness tearing at her. "How can I?"

Jane shrugged. "I guess that's something you'll have to decide on your own. But I'm a great example of someone who loves it here. It is easy to adapt to the hardships, and I'm fortunate because Algernon has seen where I come from, understands what women do and can accomplish there, and tries every day to help me achieve more here." Her eyes turned misty and to Eva, it was obvious the love they shared. For a moment she was filled with a happy sort of heart-filled envy. She didn't resent Jane her good fortune, just desperately wished for the same.

And why couldn't she have it? She sighed.

Lord Hereford approached. "Why the sad sigh? When I left her in your capable hands, Duchess, she was happy."

Jane grinned. "I think she must be missing your company, for I've done my best."

"Then I'm happy to oblige with my arm and my handsome smile." He over exaggerated a ridiculous face with a large toothy grin.

Jane and Eva laughed, and the duke arrived in that moment. "Gah! What is this expression! You look as though you've had a sour bit of something that disagrees!"

"Never you mind. For now, we are off to the boats."

"Are we to take one to the opposite shore?"

"Certainly, where our carriage awaits."

"How exciting." Jane took her husband's arm, and Eva took Lord Hereford's, and for a moment she felt as though all was right in the world.

They approached the boats. People lined up along the edge, stepping down into boats that took them out into the river. When it was their turn, Eva stepped down the first two steps when a man held out his hand to help steady her as she stepped into the craft.

But Lord Hereford reached forward and said, "Allow me." He braced himself on shore and held her hand, steadying her as she stepped out over the rim of what looked like a wobbly boat. Truly, she'd hopped on plenty of ski boats in her life and felt like she could manage on her own even, but who knew what would happen in her dress and slippers? Also, it was lovely to feel so cared for by another. She couldn't think of a time when she was so much the attention of another person, more precisely, another man. The heady feeling of being noticed and by one she'd like to cherish forever was almost more than she could manage. She hurried and sat near the rear of the boat.

Lord Hereford helped Jane over the side, the duke followed, and the three of them joined her.

"This is incredible. I've always wondered how they managed it. The women all in dresses, the men in their hessians. It seemed terribly complicated in the books and pictures..." She bit her tongue, but Lord Hereford didn't seem to notice, and the duke winked at her.

The duke cleared his throat. "You never know what will go down in history as being remembered. The smallest thing might be taken in memory by someone—a painting on a wall, or in a ballroom could be hanging in a museum someday."

Lord Hereford eyed him but said nothing.

Jane and the duke shared a small and secretive smile, and Eva again wondered at their story. The rest of their story. How did they meet? How did they come to be living here? Why England and not 2020 America? It seemed a no brainer to her. But then, she didn't have a dukedom to worry about. Someday perhaps she'd hear it all in its entirety.

They made their way across the river and down around the bend. Lord Hereford sat as close to her as possible, their legs pressed against each other, his arm across the back of their bench. She appreciated his strength and the warmth his body provided. The wind had picked up on the river and she felt a bit cold.

He pointed across the way. "And that is Buckingham house. The queen spends most of her time there. The king had it built as a home for their family."

"Oh, I'm so glad you pointed that out." She craned her neck to see across the grounds. "Are those the royal parks?"

"In a manner of speaking. If you look, you can see St. James. And of course, Westminster."

"Are the house of lords in session?"

"Not at the moment, no."

"Are you much involved?"

The admiration on his face was so pointed, she wanted to look away. "I don't think a woman has ever asked me any question about my role in the house of lords. But I am, yes. I sit in session with the lords when we meet."

"What are the issues you are discussing right now?"

"We are in recess at the moment. But right before we adjourned, we were discussing the corn laws and the many ways in which our poor suffer."

"Oh, that is so important. Do you know how much they really suffer? Have you considered that they have no manner in which to care for themselves, to provide for their own food and to obtain work? And we must consider the women. What do they do if unmarried when their fathers pass away? Who cares for them? Not just the nobility but the poor as well? And—"

Jane cleared her throat.

Eva's gaze flicked over to Jane and back to Lord Hereford. His gaze was intent as always, but a flash of concern lingered in his expression. What had he to be concerned about? These were serious problems in his country, and he in a position to do something.

"Anyway, I apologize for going on, but have you considered in this very law that raising the tax on corn might be harmful to your citizens?"

His mouth dropped. "How could you know?"

"Know what?"

The duke looked away, hiding his grin but Jane wacked him on the arm and frowned at Eva.

"That the corn will be taxed higher."

She sighed. "I don't know. I suppose I heard it somewhere."

"She read it."

"Oh yes, was that it?"

"Certainly. There was a cartoon in the paper discussing this very thing. We left the paper on the table in the breakfast room."

"Oh, right. Yes. I'm certain that's it." Eva looked away. What was her role? Did she try to influence a bit of change while she was here? She'd read about the situation for the poor in England right now. They were destitute and growing tired of it. Soon they would begin rallies and demonstrations. The Tories in England would have to come to grips with the incorrectness of their stance and make some changes. And the corn law was one big trigger that got the people riled up.

Perhaps she shouldn't say anything at all. Because if she rid the people of their triggers, maybe they wouldn't rally. She pressed her lips together and swallowed back every other soap box argument that rose to her lips while they were in the boat.

Lord Hereford kept to himself as well, his gaze directed out across the water, his thoughts keeping him occupied. She could only imagine how often the thought of her unsuitability would be running through his mind. And he would be correct. She was not only ill suited to pretend to be a Regency woman for the rest of her life, she was considered reasonably feminist for a woman in the year 2020. How utterly ridiculous to confine herself to a time period when women had so few rights.

Jane scooted over closer to her. "Remember. The nobility did have a greater influence than you think. Even the women." She squeezed her hand and sat close to her the rest of the boat ride.

When they arrived at the opposite shore, Lord Hereford helped her back out of the boat, but now his expression was one of politeness and careful attentiveness, not the similar intensity she had come to expect in their charged moments together. She couldn't stem the disappointment she felt. But she didn't try to do anything to revive his fire. Or interest. It was for the best, and she knew it. She should let his feeling for her die.

But as he helped her into his carriage and came to sit beside her, he was as friendly as ever. "Let's see how many items we accomplished from your bucket list, shall we?"

"Oh. Wonderful." She opened the journal on her lap for him to peruse and as he ran his finger down the list, she realized too late what he was reading.

"Aha!" He stopped on the one item she hoped he wouldn't see.

"Kiss an earl?" Both his eyebrows raised to his hairline. "Kiss. An. Earl." Was he disappointed? Disgusted? Astonished? Most certainly.

"Um. I had hoped you wouldn't see that item."

"Hmm. Now that I have, would you mind answering a few questions?"

"I could. Perhaps."

"Is this item...still on your list? Or was it written in a moment of reckless abandon of youth?"

She looked away. Perhaps this was the moment, added onto the previous outlandishly liberal comments to really try to drive him away. If he thought her a hoyden, he couldn't possibly still be interested. "It is still one of the most important items on my list." Her eyes met his, brazen, daring, hoping to scare him away.

The maid on the opposite corner pretended not to hear.

She lifted her chin, her eyes daring his, challenging him.

When his eyes darkened, she thought for a moment he would meet her challenge. But instead, he lifted the journal onto his lap and counted off the items they'd accomplished in their day. "A visit to Vauxhall. Check. A balloon launch. Check. I'm happy to be the person who gets to check these items off with you."

"Are you?"

He looked away, his eyes troubled. And he didn't answer.

"Are you?"

When he faced her again, his eyes looked a bit too conflicted, but she waited. She wanted to know.

"I don't know."

She nodded.

"I am happy to accompany you of course, but..."

"But?"

"You push me, demand more from me, from everyone around you. Like right now, who has expected such a response? Who would try to talk and address things openly in this manner?"

She shrugged. "Me."

They pulled in front of her townhome. He climbed out to help her down. "Thank you for a wonderful afternoon in the park." He bowed smartly and led her to the front door.

The butler opened it and waited.

Eva curtseyed and turned from him without another word.

Whorn Oliver arrived home, his mother was waiting for him in the front room. "Is that you, son?"

"Yes, mother. What are you doing in here?" She had nothing with her, no needlepoint, not even a book. She sat stiffly with her hands in her lap.

"Who were you with?"

"I went to Vauxhall with the duke and duchess and their friend, Lady Eva."

"Their friend. And how do they know this friend? When none of the rest of us has ever heard of such a person as Lady Eva?"

"I don't know. From what she says, her family lives on a small estate in the north of England. Her father is a baron."

"Who we've never heard of."

He didn't admit that the same lack of knowledge of her family had concerned him as well. "I don't know, Mother. Whoever she is, she seems perfectly respectable. For the first time, I've been interested in knowing a woman better."

"What do you think of her?"

"I enjoy our time together. I'm not certain it will come of anything. But I might spend more time with her to find out."

His mother's lips pursed. "I've invited a family to come to tea tomorrow. I would like you to be there to help entertain their daughter."

"Mother, I don't need your assistance in choosing how I spend my time."

"I think you do."

"Please, Mother. She might be someone I cannot abide. And then I will be left entertaining her at balls and expected to not neglect her. Once introductions are made, once the familiarity of our home has become a part, there are expectations."

"Precisely. Please, humor your mother, if nothing else. While this Lady Eva might be intriguing for the moment, you might be wise to find someone who has been raised as you have, who understands the workings of the ton, your expectations in the House of Lords, someone who can complete you and make you happy as well as knows how to run a proper estate."

Could Lady Eva run an estate? She had such outlandish views of things. He'd never been so shocked to discover she had such strong Whig tendencies. And to hear her talk passionately about subjects so decidedly beyond her understanding was at first interesting to him but then worrisome. He couldn't have her spouting off any of her thoughts to their friends and family or to other members of the house of lords.

He had to be careful how he moved forward in the current opinions that were unfolding around him. The disappointment that had fueled a disheartening sense of doom where their potential was concerned made him doubt any further potential with her. He sat down with a disheartened plop next to his mother. "Who is this woman you would like me to meet?"

She patted his knee. "Oh, thank you, son. I hoped you'd be agreeable. She's well sought after. Most men would be happy to be aligned with her and her family. Her dowry is excellent, and she's a lovely person besides. Lady Everly."

He'd seen her. What man hadn't noticed the beautiful Lady Everly? She glided across the floor, held herself in a state of elegance whenever he saw her, and she had the perfect heart shaped face with bright eyes. She was gentle and accepting and cheerful. Someone he might have considered before he'd met the delightfully unique and daring and enticing Lady Eva. But he had learned what came with the daring and enticing side to her and wondered if his family and his estate might do better with someone who wasn't so bold and, he admitted, frightening.

"She's an excellent choice, Mother."

He spent the next several hours answering correspondence. Rubbing his fingers into his temples, he thought about his mother's desire that he meet and court Lady Everly. They were to pay a call to her mother that very afternoon, and he determined to make a good impression, regardless of what came of the meeting. Once back in his rooms, he rang for his valet.

When his trusted man arrived, he held his arms out. "I'll be making calls. I think I'd rather the green jacket."

"And the Oriental perhaps?

"Yes." Oliver preferred the more traditional knots, but he knew the ladies were prone to observing knots and even commenting on the degree of elaborate fabric right below his neck. Lady Eva herself had been so fascinated she wished to watch Beau Brummel. Of all the ridiculous...

"Do you suppose Beau Brummel has created another knot?" His valet was instructed to remain current on the latest fashions in the event Oliver would ever care to know.

"He's doing a public presentation of his latest knot come Thursday."

Oliver jerked his head towards his valet, messing up the good servant's efforts. "Are you certain?"

"I am."

"Has he ever done such a thing before?"

"No, my lord."

How incredibly fortuitous that one of the items Lady Eva hoped to accomplish was coming to fruition already this week. He frowned. How could she possibly know such a thing was possible? Well, he certainly wasn't going to stand around outside Brummel's window, watching the man dress so Lady Eva could participate. He snorted. Imagine his mother's face when she found out Lady Eva was likely the only woman to do so.

But his valet most definitely should watch. "Of course, you must be in attendance."

He nodded. "Yes, my lord."

He finished up and met his mother at the bottom of the stairs.

"Oh, you do look well. I'm certain they will be most impressed."

"I hope to gain their good favor for more than my cravat."

"Yes, of course. But you know a woman looks with her eyes first, her heart second."

He wasn't certain his mother was accurate, nor did he want her to be. Surely the whole lot of them, men and women, were much more concerned with matters of the mind *and* heart? But he knew his hope founded on only the wishes of a flawed man, for wasn't he naturally influenced and drawn to women who were attractive to him?

He straightened his jacket as they approached the front door of Lady Everly's home. Perhaps she'd be someone he could become enamored with, someone he could make a happy life with. Thoughts of Lady Eva clouded his thinking, but he pushed them aside.

Their butler let them into the house and a footman guided them to a set of double doors. When he nodded, they opened and the servant announced, "Lord Hereford and Lady Hereford."

Lady Everly stood. Her smile was lovely and polite. Her mother stood. Three other ladies were apparently visiting and all stood, their faces somewhat flushed, their eyelashes fluttering.

All he could think about was any number of things Lady Eva might have said in that moment to bring a shocked smile to his face.

"We are so happy you stopped by." Lady Everly's mother curt-seyed and held out her hands.

Oliver's mother rushed to her and the two reminded him of young girls with their news. They turned to him, their eyes calculating and as pleased as he'd ever seen a pair of women.

"I would like to make some introductions." Oliver's mother smiled and reached her hand out to Oliver.

He stepped forward and introductions were made. When he bowed over Lady Everly's hand, his gaze flicked up to hers, but she was looking elsewhere. When he rose, her gaze was on him exclusively.

"And how are you finding the season?"

"Oh, it's lovely. My first, you know."

"I'm happy to hear it. You've made an excellent impression."

She dipped her head in mock humility and fluttered her eyelashes at him.

He offered his arm, as he knew was expected of him. They walked around the room, taking a turn. She kept her expression pleasant, passive, but said nothing.

"I wonder, might I ask something that has been on my mind of late?"

"Of course." Her smile was soft, demure, complacent.

"What are your goals?"

"Goals?" For the first time, she appeared flustered.

"Yes, a list perhaps, of things you'd like to accomplish?"

She colored slightly, and he inwardly celebrated that he'd unsettled her. For he'd love to see what Lady Everly was made of. And how would she compare to his ever-transparent Lady Eva.

"Oh, well." She looked away. "I suppose I would like to finish my needlepoint this week and work on my painting."

"I see. And where were you hoping to visit this week? The opera perhaps?"

She brightened at that. "Oh, I would dearly love to attend the opera."

"Then it is decided. We shall go together, if I might be so bold as to invite you and your mother to join us in our box?"

"Of course, thank you." Her demure expression returned, but if he looked closely, hints of pleasure lit her face here and there, the tiniest crinkle next to her eye, the turn of her mouth, her hand pressing more into his forearm.

They returned to their seats, and Lady Everly's mother served tea. All in all, Oliver thought the visit a success. He'd acquired a meeting at the opera. His mother would be proud. But for all the celebrations he would like to attempt, he couldn't shake the feeling that perhaps no matter how he tried, Lady Everly would never fascinate him as much as Lady Eva already had.

🦋 13 🦋

Eva tried to tell herself she didn't care whether or not Lord Hereford attended Almack's that evening. She was thrilled at an invitation, no doubt acquired because of her friendship with the duke and duchess. How would it be in this time period without so elevated a friendship? She imagined not nearly as enjoyable. Lady Anna again chose to stay at home. Eva suspected she was missing Trent.

Jane sat, pressed to her side. "Have I told you yet how much I enjoy that you and I can see eye to eye on certain things?"

"Yes, your grace. You've mentioned it." The duke's wry smile made Eva laugh. "But I daresay, your husband also understands much of what we see."

"Much, but not all."

"We've come to an agreement, a middle ground so to speak, haven't we?" His hopeful smile was too charming.

Eva nodded to them both. "I can see clearly that you have. If only I could find something as well-worked and enjoyable as the two of you have managed, even with such a great distance between your birthplace and customs."

The servants were no doubt constantly in a confusion about what their employers could possibly be talking about. But Eva respected the need to maintain secrecy about Twickenham and the many opportunities available at such a magical place.

"So, who should I dance with this evening?"

"I shall acquire all the necessary introductions for you. The hottest item this season is of course, Lord Hereford."

"Is he?" She tried to suppress the excitement. "Do you think he'll attend?"

"I imagine he has reasons for attempting to make an appearance."

The duke snorted. "Men don't enjoy Almacks quite as much as the ladies do, I'm afraid. Unless they are actively seeking a wife. House parties or private balls provide much more enjoyment, without so much structure and watching eyes." He wiggled his hands.

"I see." Eva frowned. "And you must point out the patronesses. One will attend, don't you think?"

"They're all here, usually. Though I haven't noticed, to be honest." Jane shrugged. "But I'll show you their venerable selves."

"Thank you." She smiled. Two bucket list items accomplished in one evening, perhaps. Swipe a souvenir from one of the patronesses. She laughed, and she thought of Lord Hereford's laugh.

"Oh dear, and what devious plans have you just created in that active mind of yours?" The duke raised an eyebrow.

"Nothing at all. I'm simply looking forward to a lovely, memorable, evening."

Jane nodded. "Just so you know, part of our history happened at just such an event and a painting made of Algernon here."

Eva looked from one to the other, but they laughed to themselves and didn't seem anxious to share.

When they were at last entering the ballroom, Eva relished the soft flipping of her stomach as she anticipated her evening. "Everyone is so beautiful." The people danced, weaving around each other, dresses swirling, faces laughing. The walls were lined with couples talking and laughing, with chaperones looking anxiously or hopefully on.

"This is going to be a night to remember, I'm sure of it."

Jane sidled up to her. "As far as other men to be made aware, would you like to know the disreputable sorts as well as the marriageable ones?"

"The disreputable might be best, since I can't offer much by way of marriage."

"And your heart is already taken in that regard."

She sucked in her breath. "Is it?"

"Why yes, of course. If you were free to stay, do you not agree?"

She considered Lord Hereford and began to nod in agreement before she shook her head. "How could I possibly know? We have barely conversed."

Jane smiled. "Sometimes it doesn't take much more than a moment or two."

Their names were announced and most of the eyes in the room lifted in their direction.

"Wow." Eva had never been the very center of attention before.

"Just smile and enjoy yourself. This might be your only Almacks ball."

The thought brought such a sadness to her, she determined even more to make the most of her time. "Too true. Find me the handsomest rake in the room."

"Okay. Here we go."

Eva was introduced to half the men in the room, her dances almost taken in completion before they approached Lord Grenville.

Jane smiled and curtseyed. "May I present Lady Eva to your lordship?"

His smile lifted at the corner, and he appraised her from head to toe. "You might, indeed. Who is this lovely new contender?"

"Contender?" Eva tilted her head in question, and Jane nearly laughed out loud.

He stepped closer. "Or perhaps she is unconquerable?" He lifted her hand to his mouth. "I'd love to dance with such a woman."

His gaze stared deep into her own, and even though she knew him to be a master player in the most expert sense, she felt her temperature rise. She dipped her head. "I have a set free. My fifth from now."

"So many taken?" He placed her hand on his arm. "I should have known and been the first to approach you as you entered. My eyes have been drawn to you, following your every step since then."

"Oh." She smiled, and Jane laughed.

"I see you've found a comfortable arm to rest upon while waiting your first set." She curtseyed and Eva could only shake her head.

"Is she your chaperone this evening?"

"Of a sort. I don't hold much to the need for such things." Her gaze turned suggestive. Perhaps if Lord Hereford would be off limits, this lord could help check the kissing box. His hair styled in a wave on top of his head, his jawline sharp against his cravat, his jacket fit to perfection and his breeches, when she dared let her eyes wander, were just right.

Lord Hereford's face flashed through her mind, and she felt twinges of guilt. But she tried to stamp those feelings away. Why should she hold to the same morality as prescribed in such an outdated time? What was a kiss to most people in her day? A friendly greeting. It's not as though she were committing to marriage or anything, and besides, this man was a rake.

He probably kissed as many women as would allow it. And besides, Lord Hereford need never know.

In the meantime, Lord Grenville stood closer, his breath tickling her neck. "In that case, I have just become *your* most avid contender."

She wanted to be enamored with this incredibly handsome man who was so interested in her, or rather a dalliance with her. "Perhaps I shall need a bit of fresh air."

She felt eyes from the opposite wall watching her. She lifted her gaze, and to her surprise Lord Hereford's frown penetrated across the room straight to her throat it seemed, choking her next words. A new lady clung to his arm in a proprietary manner, and Eva wondered why he could even feel the need to censor her associations if he too was entertaining others.

Mr. Alcott approached. She'd agreed to a dance with him. Lord Grenville held her hand as long as possible as he passed her over to this new person.

"Are you and Lord Grenville...friends?" Mr. Alcott seemed to be asking more with those few words than were stated. Did he wonder if she was, "That kind of girl?" Such an interesting time to live.

"No, I just happened to meet him this evening. I believe we will have a dance later."

"Ah, very good." He stood taller and behaved as every proper man would. They danced a form of the waltz. She'd never seen it before, but it was easy enough to pick up. The music moved in threes, but a group of four of them performed the steps, almost as though they were to do a Quadrille. She enjoyed it. The thought of dancing the whole evening, practicing the steps she'd learned for her re-enactments, meeting all these new people and fully immersing herself in this lifestyle thrilled her.

One of the other ladies, a Miss Harper, whispered. "Oh, that we could just dance the waltz itself. This foursome is tiring."

When Eva circled back and landed at her side, she nodded. "I so agree."

"Have you been approved yet?"

"I have." Jane had told her they'd already worked some kind of social magic, and she was free to dance the waltz openly.

"Oh, if only I could be approved." Her pout was endearing.

Eva was impressed at the training and the mannerisms of all these women, so versed in acceptable matters of deportment and speech. They were charming, every one of them, and quite lovely.

No wonder Lord Hereford was quite shocked at Eva's behavior. But he'd also seemed refreshed by it.

At any rate, he hadn't left Eva's eyesight since she left Lord Grenville's side. Every time she looked his way, he was staring. Did the lady at his side notice such a thing? Surely she must. But she stood demurely, responding with a small smile whenever he spoke to her.

At the conclusion of this set, another handsome man bowed over her hand. She couldn't remember his name, but she curtseyed and greeted him. They began the very longest dance ever made—the Quadrille.

She understood at once what the young ladies in all the books she read were complaining about when having to dance the Quadrille with an odious partner. For this new man, though not odious, was the most boring creature she'd encountered.

But as she circled, Lord Grenville brushed her shoulder a bit longer than necessary and let his hand rest in hers long past when it needed to be there. Now here was something to add some excitement to the dance.

She grinned in response and nearly laughed at his wink.

Jane waved from the corner, obviously enjoying her own entertainment all provided by Eva's first Almack's experience. Her partner leaned closer, and Eva had to look away as his breath wafted over. "You're a proficient. Excellent dancing."

"Thank you." She greatly preferred the silent and boring man with no offensive smells. As she circled back around, Lord Grenville once again took her hands. He smelled lovely, as he whispered, "Perhaps we can end this interminable dance early." A lovely clove smell filled the air around her.

All the while, Lord Hereford made her aware of every step of her foot, every lift of her hand and every smile on her face. That awareness made her long for his company. Dash it all. She grinned at her own Regency thought. But felt powerless to her situation.

At great length, the dance ended and they clapped for the musicians. Before another man could come and take their spot, Lord Grenville approached, his eyes full of expectation, but Lord Hereford approached more quickly and was at her side with her hand on his arm before she could say another word.

"Hello, my lord."

He didn't respond, though his face was stern, his eyes were full of adventure.

"Might I ask where we are going?"

He glanced at her and then kept walking, nodding here and there as they passed what she assumed were his acquaintances. When they had moved far enough to be out of earshot, he sighed. "Where are we going? Out of that blaggard's reach."

"Who?"

He raised an eyebrow.

"Lord Grenville?"

"Yes, Lord Grenville. Don't think I don't understand what you're doing."

She wished he'd never seen her bucket list. But as her eyes wandered around to make certain the man in question was truly nowhere nearby, her eyes caught one of the patroness's. She pointed, subtly. "Is that—"

"Lady Jersey. Yes."

"Perfect. I need your assistance. I know you wish to discuss my extreme lack of propriety and even perhaps your concern about my moral compass, but right now, I need to steal that lady's feather."

"P-pardon me?"

"Yes, or her handkerchief. Oh, or her fan. Something on her person that I could easily conceal on my person."

"And you wonder why I have concerns about your moral compass?"

"She has a dozen at least, I'm certain. If it appeases your own sensibilities, I'll ask the duke to buy her another to replace it."

"Then why this crazy—is this too on your list?"

She nodded. "There is another page you haven't seen."

He shook his head then eyed her, and he must have overcome an internal battle because he smiled. "What do we need to do?"

"I think, first of all, we must be in conversation with her. With perhaps some others? And you would need to be the distraction, while I work some kind of trick to get her to part with her items."

"Distraction? In what way?"

"You don't know how to distract a lady?"

His face turned red, and Eva found him even more adorable.

"I am quite adept at distracting. Perhaps you've noticed?" He held her gaze, and though she tried to look away, she couldn't manage.

"Yes, I've noticed."

"But she's not the distracting type, if you know what I mean."

Eva tried not to think about what that meant for his opinion of her own distractibility. "Oh come now, let's give this a go."

"After you."

"No, you. I have to cling to your arm in obvious fawning over your lord-ness and your money and position in society, and you have to do something unique and intelligent."

"The things you say." He glanced down at her upturned and adoring expression. "Though I will admit to liking this look on you."

She blinked, then tugged on his arm, her expression unchanging.

"Oh, bother. Whatever you do, don't drag me into your thievery."

"You will be an innocent bystander."

They approached the woman, surrounded by other women, mostly. Everyone with the same look of reverential awe. As he moved closer, they all stepped aside so that he could bow before her. Eva curtseyed and Lord Hereford introduced her.

"I'm so pleased to meet you." Eva dropped her eyes in the most demure expression she could muster.

Lady Jersey nodded regally. "And I you. I've been most intrigued by our newest arrival here in the ton. Your friends cannot speak highly enough. I do hope you do their name and estate credit while you are among us. As they've staked their reputation on your supreme acceptance here."

Eva nodded. "I would never dream of doing anything but bringing honor to my friends."

Lord Hereford stepped on her toe, just the tiniest nudge, but she couldn't believe the audacity.

And then he began the longest stream of small talk she'd ever heard. They discussed the weather, the balls, the gowns, even the hairstyles. When she began a discourse on the flavors of ice available, Eva knew that nothing in this conversation would be distracting enough for her to take even the smallest token.

Lady Jersey had four feathers coming out of the top of her turban. But those sat rather tall on her head, and Eva had no way of knowing how they were attached. Perhaps plucking them out would be much more difficult than she imagined. What else did Lady Jersey have on her person? A small reticule that was slipped over her wrist. The woman seemed aware of it and touched it often. Oh bother, what else? Perhaps her fan which she seemed to hold, absently, now and then waving it about for emphasis.

Eva had an idea.

"Lady Jersey."

She stopped mid-sentence and rose her eyebrows in Eva's direction.

"I was wondering. Have you been inside Carlton house?"

The woman's mouth pursed in such a supreme expression of dislike that Eva wondered if perhaps she'd chosen the wrong topic.

"I have, and the whole house is such a monumental waste, I'm unsure why the king allows it."

Eva wanted to mention that perhaps the king was incapable, but Prinny was not yet the regent and they were unaware of the king's state. At any rate, she continued. "I was wondering if you could explain the artwork for us?"

"Oh, I suppose I could. It was the most redemptive part of the house, to be sure."

As she began talking, Eva held out her hand. "I fear you cannot be doing it justice with this fan in your hand. Would you mind describing the sculpture's size, show us with your hands perhaps?"

Lord Hereford snorted and then coughed in to his hands. "Excuse me, yes, I too am most interested."

"Oh, well, indeed. I am pleased to find two young people so interested in the great art and artists of our day." She proceeded to hand the fan to Eva and began the longest discourse on artwork Eva had heard, indeed it rivaled that of the museum docents. And true to Eva's request, Lady Jersey used her hands with great proficiency in every description. In the meantime, Eva tucked the fan away in her own reticule.

The music started for another set, and Lord Hereford bowed. "Oh, my dear Lady Jersey. if you'll excuse us, this is the very dance I've asked Lady Eva for."

"Oh, why certainly. Do return if you'd like to hear more."

"We will."

They parted, and Lord Hereford swung her into his arms.

"What?"

"The waltz."

"Oh, so many haven't been given permission yet."

"But I assume you have."

"Certainly."

"I would dance it with no other."

As he led her about the floor, her feet gliding and then almost flying as effortlessly as she had ever danced, the air between them seemed to shimmer. Without thinking, she melted into him, the distance shrinking, her heart longing to feel the beat of his. He spun her and they twirled and moved. "You are meant to be in my arms. Can you not feel it?" His words warmed her and sent a thrill down her core.

"Yes." She breathed then started, shocked at her response. "I mean, I don't know."

"No, stop. Go with your first answer, for that was the very language of your heart telling your brain to be still."

His words rang through her. But her brain definitely needed to have a say in this conversation. Her heart might find a happy home in this man's arms. But her brain knew what staying here would lead.

But as he stared into her eyes, as they danced the floors at Almacks, as she realized she'd never met a man she trusted more. For a moment, she let herself go and just enjoyed their dance. For it would end all too soon and she would dance with another and another. But she knew always, in the back of her mind, Lord Hereford would be the standard she sought. And she didn't think anyone in this time, her time or any other time would ever compare.

14

Lord Hereford returned Lady Eva to the duke and duchess but was loathe to leave her. He knew she'd be scooped up by her next partner, knew he'd taken some man's place as her partner, but he didn't care. Every moment spent with her seemed worth the agony of those moments apart.

Her list fascinated him and filled him with dread. Would she leave with that scoundrel Grenville? Would he enjoy the taste of her lips on his? The thought caused his blood to boil. And how could he respect a woman who had as her goal to kiss a lord? How could he let her kiss another? He was a lord. He could be the one. But as a man of honor, he knew what such a gesture would mean.

He couldn't explain his attraction, but somehow, coming from her, the pursuit to kiss a lord seemed less villainous and more adventurous. As had stealing Lady Jersey's fan. Was he an accomplice now, to the thievery? He supposed not since the lady had willingly handed over her fan. At least the duchess had agreed to replace the item.

"Have you both been enjoying yourselves? I must say, I've rarely seen the waltz danced so well." Jane smiled at the two of them and Oliver appreciated her friendship.

"Yes, we are well suited." Oliver dipped his head.

But Lady Eva didn't respond, her attention was elsewhere.

He followed her gaze and nearly growled. Grenville. The man danced by them and had the audacity to wink in her direction. She smiled and then turned back to their group. "I've had a lovely time. Almacks is everything I thought it would be." She stepped closer to Oliver and whispered. "Do you know I'm well on my way to crossing off four things on this list?"

His dread increased. "Oh? Which ones?"

Her eyes danced with the adventure he knew she felt in her wild plan. "Well, you know about the fan." She patted her reticule. "I've had the lemonade. I've danced a quadrille with a boring partner." She made a face. "And of course, you know who might humor me with the item we mustn't discuss in public."

He grimaced. Then eyed her. "And the fourth?"

"Oh." She looked away. "Well, it's um…"

Jane saved her. "Shall we sit? My feet ache and I'm certain Lady Eva's suitors will find her no matter where she is."

"I would enjoy a rest, myself." Eva moved with the duke and duchess to chairs against the wall. Lord Hereford followed and glanced around the room.

"Who were you with earlier?"

A victorious smile lit his face, and she almost rolled her eyes but knew the expression meant nothing during this time period.

"Oh please, who is she?"

"I'm just counting my victories as they come. You noticed." He nodded and folded his arms.

"And I still don't know who she is."

"That, is Lady Everly. We've recently become acquainted, and our mothers are much in favor of the match."

Lady Eva's face pinched for a moment and then cleared. And Oliver wanted immediately to squelch that worry, but what could he say? As certain he was that Lady Eva was the woman he most preferred, he was unsure as yet if she was the correct woman to be his wife. She certainly had no plans to stick by his side as of yet. He had not won her over in any way. So he left the explanation as it stood. Would he live to regret the choice?

Lady Eva returned to the dance floor within minutes, and she was on the arm of one gentleman or another for the rest of the evening. At one point, he lost sight of her and had a growing suspicion she might have been with Grenville, for he was out of sight as well.

Several hours later, the room was distracted by a strange object floating above them. It looked to be a parchment, folded into the shape of a bird with wings soaring through the air above their heads. He watched it, astounded, then in great suspicion, and found Lady Eva eyeing it with a victorious expression. He caught her eye and she made a checking off motion with her finger. He couldn't help but laugh and marvel at her ingenuity.

Lady Everly had returned to his side, and he did his best to go through the motions of showing interest in the woman, but a part of him knew it to be hopeless. He was not interested in her. So did he make a decision based on matters of the mind or the heart? That would be the question he most desired to answer.

OLIVER MEANDERED DOWN THE STREET IN THE LATE afternoon the next day, enjoying a bit of solitude. The weather was lovely. The streets were dry, and few people were out promenading so he had space in which to breathe and to think.

Up ahead, a carriage pulled in front of a shop, and Lady Eva and Her Grace stepped out and hurried in.

He picked up his pace, all designs of solitude gone. He arrived at the shop door, opened it and stepped inside. Strong scents filled his nose. As his eyes adjusted to the dim lighting, he recognized tables and shelves of the familiar oils and waters they used to scent their baths or to wear on their clothing or other places. He'd never actually been in a store that sold the items. His valet handled the purchase of his.

Lady Eva stood in the corner, lifting the different vials to her nose and laughing with her grace. "This one would never fly. Smell this."

Her grace took one smell and said, "Oh that's all the rage here. Prinny wore it once and now all the men think it makes them smell like Drakkar."

"Oh, Drakkar. They could use some Drakkar around here."

"I brought some back with me last time."

"What! You did!"

She giggled. "Totally. And a bunch of other stuff. Regency's not so bad when you can cheat a little bit."

Oliver could not make sense of anything they said, but as he moved closer, his hip jiggled a table and rows of vials jingled and clanged together.

Lady Eva's eyes widened and she nudged her grace. "Hello, Lord Hereford."

"Hello." He bowed and they curtseyed. "What gibberish are you speaking? I could scarce understand a word."

Lady Eva laughed. "Oh, you know, we women have our own language sometimes."

"And what is this Drakkar?"

They eyed each other, and then he knew one would try to hedge. They were hiding something, something they seemed to share in common. "Are you two from the same place?" Her grace too had come and joined the ton from a distant family estate.

Lady Eva nodded. "We are. And it has been so enjoyable to talk again of things from home."

Something still seemed odd between the two of them, but at last a portion of the mystery was explained. "And now, here we all are together. Shall we pick a new smell for the other?"

Lady Eva's eye lit. "How perfectly spontaneous of you, Lord Hereford."

"You approve of spontaneous?"

"Certainly." She rested a hand on his arm and her grace joined him on his other arm. "Now, let's see what we can choose for you."

They headed to the men's section of the store, and after smelling four or five vials, Lady Eva breathed in one and her smile of enjoyment made him grin. He peered over her shoulder immediately to see what had caused such a reaction.

Her grace smelled it next. "Ooh, I like that one. Perhaps I'll get it for his grace."

Lady Eva handed it to him next. He lifted it to his nose. "Earth. Woods. Rain." He turned eyes to her. "This smells good to you?"

"So good." She lifted it to her nose again. "When I smell this, I think of beautiful nights with the man I love holding me, his hand, here." She placed his hand at her hip. "And the fire warm, a slow dance, and a soft kiss..." She sighed.

He closed his mouth after his lips went dry. "I'd like to purchase a few, if I may?" He reached around her and picked up the desired vials.

"And now, shall we find one for you?"

Eva nodded. "This is fun."

They led him to another section of the store. He picked up vial after vial and none of them would do. One was too sweet, one too strong, one too much like the one he held. He moved down the aisles, one after another until at last, he smelled one that matched Lady Eva. "This. Jasmine. To me it smelled of flowers I'd only encountered in a green house or conservatory."

She lifted it hesitantly to her nose. "Oh. Mmm. I love this." She checked the label. "Jasmine. Of course."

"You like it, then?"

"I do."

He waited, hoping she would buy it. For he most desperately wished to smell it on her. She was about to place it back on the table when he moved to reach for it.

"So I should buy it, then?" Eva lifted it closer.

"Absolutely. The thought of this smell right here." He ran a finger from the base of her ear down to the base of her neck. "Sounds delicious to me."

She stood back in complete pleased surprise. "Lord Hereford."

He shrugged and handed her two vials. Perhaps he was bold, but she seemed to welcome his sincerity, or perhaps her own boldness brought out his.

Then she laughed and they both moved to the counter to make their purchases. The women had to leave soon after, and as he helped them up into their carriage, he could only smile at the expectant looks Lady Eva sent his way. Perhaps there might be hope for them after all?

THE NEXT FEW DAYS WERE FULL OF SENSELESS AND DULL activities of his mother's choosing and mostly involving the accompanying of Lady Everly here or there. They took a ride in his phaeton. They walked along the paths of Hyde Park. They went together to see the artwork in the museum. And he began to be concerned as the more his mother arranged for them to be together, the greater the expectation that he would soon make his intentions known. Of which he had none at the moment. His intention had been to decide if he had an intention. And as yet, he had no further plans where Lady Everly was concerned.

Perhaps because of his dull and relentless schedule, he found himself eagerly traversing the streets with his valet, to join the others in watching Beau Brummel get his cravat tied. He shook his head in his own dismay. And he hoped that not one of his friends would see him. But his eyes eagerly searched the crowds of people hoping to catch one particular shiny blonde-haired beauty.

He crowded in with the young bucks, many in their first season, most not titled. All hoping to add themselves to the list of truly distinguished gentlemen, or at least to appear so to the ladies. And so they watched in rapt attention as Beau pranced in front of his bay window, making the most ridiculous show about something so simple as his own dress.

But Oliver searched the crowd, and the more gentlemen who showed up the more disheartened he felt that Lady Eva would not make an appearance.

But then, when Oliver was about to give up, after Beau had fiddled with the same knot five times and forced his patient valet to re-tie this new and overly complicated knot, his eyes found her. And he laughed out loud.

Everyone turned to look at him, and he ignored them all.

Lady Eva stood on the edge of the crowd, up on the toes of her boots, wearing a ridiculous oversized bonnet, a coat twice the size of her and large ribbons tying the bonnet in place which nearly covered her face.

He approached from behind. "Where is Lady Eva, I wonder? For no one here looks anything like her…"

She whipped her head around in surprise and then a mock scowl filled her face. "Oh, be quiet, you. No one else here can tell it is I."

"I wouldn't be too certain of that. But why the costume?"

"Do you think I want people knowing the duchess's dearest friend was at the Beau Brummel presentation unaccompanied?"

He felt his mouth drop in shock. "You're unaccompanied?"

"You heard me." She turned away. "Now hush. You're interrupting one of my bucket list items. This man is a hoot, or rather, he is vastly amusing, don't you think so?"

"I think he's a ridiculous fop, but most men of the ton and their valets follow his fashion advice to the letter. My own valet is here. Which is why I should not be."

"Then why are you?" Her eyebrow raised in a delicious enticing wiggle, and he had the oddest desire to place his lips upon it.

But instead he searched her face. "Why am I here?" He stepped closer, peering in at her under her bonnet rim. "Because I knew if I came, I just might see you."

Her mouth opened into an 'o,' and her eyes widened and then she whispered. "Well here I am."

"And unaccompanied."

She turned from him. "I don't understand what that signifies."

"How can I accompany you, if you are unaccompanied?"

She shook her head and waved him away. "I have no time for your sensibilities."

"My attention to the moral strictures of our day?"

"Precisely. If you cannot accompany an unaccompanied woman, then what is the point of being a gentleman?"

He started to respond, but then had nothing more to say. She was perfectly right. As a gentleman, it was his duty to see her home.

"Shall we be off, then?"

"What? I haven't finished…" She took one more look at Beau pulling out the attempts at a new knot and turned back to him. "Ready when you are."

"You say the most curious things."

"Oh, right. Shall we be off then?"

He nodded, then indicated his valet should stay. "Shall we walk?"

"All the way home?"

"Well you cannot very well sit in my carriage with me alone, can you?"

"Again, you'd rather walk yourself into a new set of blisters than simply sit in a carriage with a woman?"

"It's your own reputation at stake."

"And I find I don't bother too much with cares for my reputation."

He shook his head. "But such a thing is preposterous. Of course you must care for your reputation. It is the most precious thing you have."

She blinked three times and still could not think of an appropriate manner in which to respond to such a ludicrous statement. One more proof that she and Lord Hereford were incredibly mismatched. And that she could never possibly live in this time period full of such backward thinking.

But then he waved and his carriage came forward.

"What? Where was it?"

"Just across the street there."

"And you don't mind riding alone with me?"

"If you are quite prepared for the consequences, then I find I'm not at all concerned." Still, he looked up and down the street three times before he joined her, and he made certain to shut the window coverings.

"You are rather too nervous about a simple ride home."

"I cannot understand how you don't feel the same degree of concern."

She settled into his seat, and he had to admit the sudden closeness of the carriage, the intimacy of such an enclosed space, filled him with possibilities. He moved to sit beside her. "See now. A ride in a carriage alone even with a gentleman can be quite scandalous."

She looked up into his face. "It might be."

"Might it not?"

"Depends what you find as scandalous." She reached into her reticule and pulled out the jasmine smelling water.

His heart picked up and the corner of his mouth lifted in a small smile. She opened up the lid and dabbed her finger. The carriage filled with the delicious sweet floral smell, and then she ran her finger down her neck from the base of her earlobe to the curve at her neckline.

Oliver watched the moisture dry against her skin and then looked back up into her face. "And now you smell as enticing as I've ever seen you appear."

"A scandal indeed."

He moved closer, his mouth and nose breathing in the delicious smell of her skin mixed with this new water. He ran his finger down the same trail following with his nose, puffing a trail of air along the path as well.

"You are as beguiling here in this carriage as you are in any place I encounter your fascinating self. But here, there is no one but yourself to stop me from placing my lips everywhere I wish them to be." He lowered his mouth so that it hovered just above her skin, so close that he could almost taste her, almost press his mouth. If she moved even a hair, his mouth would be upon her and he would have been lost to her spell.

But she closed her eyes, waiting, until he sighed and moved away. "And there you see the potential for scandal."

She nodded, her breath coming faster than usual.

"And I might have to move to this side of the carriage so as not to respond to that look in your eyes. Might I call on you, Lady Eva? Might I speak to the duke to make my intentions known?"

She nodded in a dizzy spell of happiness, or so it seemed, and then her eyes widened in concern. "I don't feel that is necessary, as yet. For we don't know what our intentions will be yet, do we? It is so early, we having just met..."

"What more is there to know than the thought that I cannot bear to part from you, and when we are together, I can only just barely keep myself from kissing you senseless?"

She turned away, a small smile on her lips. "You say the most wonderful things. I could sit back and listen to you forever." She sighed. "But we must wait. For intentions to be made known. I'm not ready for that. Lord Hereford, we don't know the first thing about each other. Call on me every day if you like. I think we'd all enjoy the company."

He could not understand such a woman, but he agreed to do so.

The carriage stopped in front of the duke's townhome. Jane came rushing out and peered in the window. "I should have known it was you."

"I promise that until I met Lady Eva, I had never once encountered a woman alone, nor had I delivered her to her home unaccompanied."

"And that I can most readily believe." The duchess smiled at him. "Do come call on us tomorrow."

He dipped his head. "Of that you can be certain."

She laughed. Eva exited and stood beside her as they waved good bye while the carriage made its way back down the street.

❧ 15 ❧

Eva prepared for the opera in the most stunning dress she had ever seen. She'd added some of her own touches to the dress, modern ideas that would still look appropriate in a Regency gown. The main color of the gown was a rich navy blue, but the fabric had a shimmer to it she loved. Then she'd asked for a lace overlay in gold color. Woven into the overlay were jewels and flowers. The stitching was stunning in and of itself. She'd had them place matching jewels and stitching on the tips of her slippers so that when her toe poked out it would sparkle in the light and add a hint of beauty. The ribbon along her décolleté was an actual weave of three colors, blue, gold and silver. She'd asked them to create a mock train that flowed from the back of her gown to the floor. Everywhere she could, she added embellishment. And she determined to enjoy her time at the opera.

She couldn't imagine an evening to be more excited for.

Her maid placed jewels in her hair. Once the maid was finished and Eva was left to herself for a moment, she applied the barest touch of her favorite lip color and then a liberal amount of her jasmine water. She might not see Lord Hereford, but if she did, she wanted to be prepared.

She was a mess. She knew it. But what was she to do? She was falling for an earl in the nineteenth century. And the more she fell, the more she wondered if she could make it work to live in a time utterly not her own. Jane and Algernon seemed blissfully happy. Her heart pounded in fear at the thought. To live here, forever?

When she and the duke and duchess descended from their carriage, she felt like a star with paparazzi all around. People crowded toward their carriage, everyone craning their necks to see her and her friends.

"Is this normal?"

The duke smiled and nodded to someone nearby. "Yes, at the opera. The audience here is varied and includes some we never see among our peers. They tend to be curious."

"They just want to look at Algernon. I don't blame them. He's hot in his breeches."

Eva snorted. "It's so odd to hear you talk like that here."

"You'll get used to it." Algernon grinned. "I do. And then I must remember to guard my own tongue depending on who we see."

"I can imagine. It's nice you've been to the future. You know where she's coming from. I think that helps."

Her two friends exchanged glances, but she ignored them and their matchmaking ways. She lifted her chin and smiled at everyone around them. "This is lovely."

"That dress." Jane fanned her face. "You will start a whole new trend, mark my words. It's stunning."

"I need to thank you for funding my wardrobe. I must say, the future is missing a decent modiste."

"Or in my case, the funds to have clothes custom made."

Eva nodded. She had made use of a personal tailor before. But why do such a thing unless making red carpet appearances? And it somehow did not seem half as cool as her trips to the modiste had been. It was so odd to think of her life at home that the world almost jarred to a stop. Too confusing to attempt to live in two realities at once, she pushed thoughts of home aside and renewed her plans to enjoy what time she had in the Regency world.

They walked inside the opera house and the crush of the crowd seemed less for a moment.

"Our boxes are up this way, but we can linger a moment if you'd like to address your fans." Algernon's eyebrows wiggled in a ridiculous fashion.

"*Your* fans, you mean." Eva indicated the crowd of people off to his left, hovering nearby. "Do they need an introduction? Why are they not approaching?"

"Because the duke must address them first. They are of the class and rank that they cannot approach without being summoned."

Eva watched the people all around them, fascinated with their rules and status fixations. "I suppose we have similar functions, though not as strongly pronounced. It would be rude for someone to step into a conversation and begin speaking to people they didn't know."

"I suppose." Jane shrugged. "All of societal rules are in strong function here."

Eva noticed the duke did not deign to converse with any of those huddling to his left. She didn't ask, knowing he must have his reasons. But it also gifted them with some space, breathing room, and a lovely view of the opera hall. So Eva was grateful.

A commotion rumbled through the crowd, making its way toward them. A man entered from the stairs.

"Beau Brummel." Jane lifted a hand, and he smiled when he saw them. As he made his way closer, the crowd noise grew louder, all heads now turned in their direction.

"This is so exciting!" Eva wished for a fan. Too bad she hadn't brought the one she borrowed. She snorted at the thought.

Beau bowed before them. "Your grace. Your grace, and..." His voice rose in question while he appraised Eva.

"This is Lady Eva, our dear friend from the north. And this is Mr. Beau Brummel."

Eva dipped low and gracefully. "Your reputation precedes you. I'm honored by an acquaintance."

He pressed his lips to her gloved knuckle. "And I you. I was drawn to your dress from across the room. I've never seen a woman so finely appointed, who carried herself so well, and who understands fashion to the degree that you obviously do. I bow to you again and applaud your choices this evening." He commenced the deepest bow.

Jane lifted a hand to her mouth, and Algernon's eyes popped in amazement.

People all around them gasped and the news spread from group to group around the room.

When Mr. Brummel arose, she curtseyed in return. "You do me a great honor. Thank you."

"I am pleased to have at last met someone who understands fashion choices as I do."

She found her words choked in her throat. She could have never predicted such a thing to occur, to appear on her bucket list. And now that it had, who did she have to share it with? No one at home. She exchanged looks with Jane and could see they were just as flummoxed as she.

They chatted with him for many minutes, and then he took his leave. "I have others I agreed to meet tonight. Perhaps I might call and we together could discuss our common preferences?"

"I would be honored." She curtseyed again and watched him make his way across the room to a group of men who immediately crowded to hear him.

"I don't know what to say." Eva shook her head.

Most of the women eyed her with partially concealed envy and others with calculating expressions.

"We will very shortly see many forms of imitation of this very dress."

"I'd imagine so."

Algernon laughed. "I must know. I have to hear from your own lips. Our dear Lord Hereford went to watch the man tie a cravat this week?"

"He did. He sent his valet to learn as well. But we left soon after. I think in the moment Mr. Brummel was retying his cravat for the sixth attempt was the point of his lapsed interest."

"Just so." Algernon straightened his back. "Shall we find our box?"

"Oh yes!" Eva attempted to walk stately behind the duke and his wife, to mimic their stance and bearing, but her feet bounced more and her excitement bubbled over until she was barely containing her desire to talk to those around her.

They pulled the curtains aside and moved to the front row seats in his box. Eva looked out over the theater. Across the way, level with her eyesight was a row of boxes. And then down below the seats were filling up.

"That's the riff raff." Jane laughed. "Can you believe that orchestra seats are where the poor sit?"

"Not exactly the poor, are they?" The duke indicated the people sitting on the main floor.

They were clean and comely. But none were in the finery Eva had grown accustomed to seeing at the social events of the ton.

"I just want to take it all in. I should have brought my camera, or my phone, anything. Now I just have to hope I remember."

"Or you could come back. Any full moon you are always welcome to stay with us." Jane fanned herself. "Though next time you come, could you lug an air conditioner?"

Eva laughed. "And some electricity?"

"Oh, right." She sighed. "But it really is worth it. I would never change a thing."

Eva considered her and Algernon as they shared looks of adoration. She appreciated what they had and wished she had something similar.

Her gaze caught on Lord Hereford, sitting directly across the way. His mother sat at his side and Lady Everly was on his other side.

"Well, look who's here tonight."

Jane followed Eva's gaze and clucked. "She's one of the most sought after debutantes. His mother is smart to bring her to his attention."

"I think he's of half a mind to pursue her himself."

"The other half wonders how to win you over."

She hoped that was true. And then felt terrible for hoping such a thing. For how could she entertain desires to win the heart of someone she would eventually have to break? Unless she made the leap...

She watched the interactions in Lord Hereford's box. His eyes remained glued to Eva, except for moments when he responded to his mother or shifted to address something with Lady Everly. And she felt the heat of his interest across the space in between.

She closed her eyes, remembering their moments in the carriage. She'd never wanted a kiss more than in their time together. But she knew such a thing would have to come from him. She would not compromise him in that way. She knew men were much more loose with their morals than women were allowed to be, but she also knew if he were to kiss her, he would be making a promise. He did not seem like the type to participate in a dalliance.

Too bad, since at this point, she predicted she'd always have at least one remaining bucket list item unfulfilled. She hadn't even thought about Lord Grenville since the night at Almack's. Though, she couldn't imagine pursuing him just to get a kiss. She supposed she had her own set of Regency morals. And she was happy about that.

But now that Lord Hereford sat across from her, with his attention solely on her, she wasn't sure she'd even notice the opera.

Jane fanned herself. "It's getting warm in here, and I'm not even getting scorching looks from hot earls across the way."

"Where's a hot earl?" The duke's mock frown made Eva laugh and then he noticed Lord Hereford. "Ah, yes."

The opera was about to begin and as the lights dimmed, she forced her eyes to watch the stage. As soon as the curtains rose, she was enchanted. She almost forgot Lord Hereford. Almost.

During a passionate scene of great angst in the performance, her gaze wandered to him and he was looking as steadfastly as always. And then he jerked his head to the side. He'd moved so that he sat on the end, Lady Everly and his mother deep in what looked like quiet conversation. And he jerked his head again. Then he rose to stand.

A deep thrill of excitement rumbled through her.

Did she dare?

Of course.

But should she? She didn't think for more than two more breaths before she stood, winked at Jane, and then snuck out the back curtain. She turned in the direction his head had indicated, rushing through the darkened and quiet area behind the boxes until she saw him approaching, his quiet steps towards her racing her blood.

He reached a hand and held a finger to his lips. They hurried together around the next bend in the circular area where he led her to a small alcove window, with a curtain across the opening. As the fabric enclosed them in such an intimate space, she held her breath. "Lord Hereford..."

He pulled her to him, gazing down into her face, his mouth inches from her own. "I couldn't wait until intermission, couldn't stand to see you in front of all the others, only able to smile and nod and politely discuss the weather. I cannot abide only casually knowing you. I wish to make you a part of every intense thought and language of my life, I wish you to be a part of every minute of my day. I want you to be mine, body and soul."

Were her ears deceiving her? Eva could scarcely believe what he had just said. Is this what her heart wanted?

"Wh-What are you saying?"

This was bound to be the most romantic moment of her life. Her eyes adjusted to the darkness, and she searched this handsome lord's face and saw only the kind intensity she'd always known. He was a good man. She was half in love with him.

"I—I'm not saying anything in particular...yet. Except for what I did say. I long for tomorrow and the next day and the next when I can call on you." He closed the distance so that their lips were almost touching, almost. And he whispered. "And I long to kiss you."

She parted her lips, feeling his soft breath as a caress on her mouth. If she lifted onto her toes, if she stood just a touch taller...

The world had gone quiet. The magic she always hoped to feel surrounded them in their small space. His arms cradled her protectively, and she breathed in the lovely smell they'd chosen for him from the shop earlier. Their combined smells, their euphoric desire, their joint understood effort to delay gratification created such a beautiful scene of intense longing. She was without words, frozen in a beautiful ecstasy unlike she'd ever known.

Then someone ripped open the curtains. Hands went over mouths, and shocked gasps filled the hallway. Eva was tempted to roll her eyes and pull the curtain back to where it had been, but Lord Hereford stepped away in horror as though she were a pariah, and shook his head.

Eva searched the crowd for a familiar face, but finding none, she pushed through those who were blocking her way, ran through the remaining groups and pushed herself back through and into the duke's box.

Jane took one look at her and rushed forward with her arms out. "What has happened?"

Noise from the conversation outside her box heightened. "...caught with Lord Hereford."

Jane nodded. "So you've created a scandal? During your first month here?" She laughed. "I'd expect nothing less."

"But I don't think Lord Hereford's amused. You should have seen his face."

"No, he wouldn't be. The man's as staid and proper as they come."

"His mother is going to throw fits. And I would pay a lot to see Lady Everly's face."

Her two friends were highly entertained, but Eva could only feel a rising dread. Lord Hereford's face had told her all she needed to know. Being caught as they had been had ruined their chance to fall well and truly in love. His face said what she hoped his words never would. He was forced to take his own action and when faced with the very real challenge of asking for her hand, he wasn't looking forward to it. At least his expression had spoken his dread as clearly as anything.

The duke approached the curtain. "Let's wait until the crowd clears and then I'll prepare my study for a young earl to come calling."

"Oh, but that is terrible."

"Is it so terrible?" Jane's face asked an honest question that Eva didn't know how to answer.

"I think I should make my way back to Twickenham."

"What? No." Jane shook her head. "Wait and see what comes of this. You've likely just earned yourself a marriage proposal, for one."

"But that's exactly what I don't want. Can't you see? And he's not too excited about the prospect of being forced to marry me, either."

"How can you even know that? I suspect he's the happiest man at the opera right now."

The three of them looked across the way at the earl's box. He was in a hushed and hurried conversation with Lady Everly, his mother standing nearby. If her looks could kill, all three of them and every commoner in between would have fainted dead away. "Well, I know for certain I've made one enemy while here."

"She'll get over it." Jane started, watched the woman for a moment and then shook her head. "No. I don't think she shall."

Lord Hereford did not look back in her direction even one more time. As soon as the music began, the three of them, of one mind, stood and made their way out of the box.

❧ 16 ❧

Oliver could not decide how to feel.

His feet dragged on a walk for some air after a long Shakespearean-like tragic monologue from his mother; but once out of sight of his house, his pace picked up and he found himself humming. Married to Lady Eva. He couldn't think of a more delightful prospect.

But he'd embroiled them both in a scandal the size of which the ton would enjoy for many months. He'd well and truly ruined her reputation, and right on the heels of Beau Brummel's unmitigated support. She went from stardom to outcast in the matter of one act at the opera. And it was his fault.

His pace kept up and he distracted himself with all the manners in which he would propose. "My dear Eva, if I might call you so?"

"Eva, my love..."

"Would you do me the great honor..."

A voice cleared.

Oliver's face whipped around and breathed out in relief. "Algernon."

They approached and clapped each other on the back.

"I'm on my way to see you."

"We suspected as much." The duke's face was troubled, foreboding.

"What has happened? Is Lady Eva well?"

"I presume she is as healthy as she ever was."

"You presume?"

"She's left us, gone back to her home, or is en route, at any rate."

The world spun in a crazy whirl. "No." He took off running toward the duke's house, but Algernon called him back.

"I have a letter. She's gone, man."

Oliver returned, out of breath. "A letter, you say?"

Algernon held out a folded paper, with a new crest he'd never seen.

"I'm sorry."

Oliver barely heard. He tore open the crest, his eyes devouring the page.

DEAR LORD HEREFORD,

I regret to inform you that I have left. I couldn't bear the nonsense I brought you by our being discovered. And so to avoid the scandal that would likely surround us were I to stay, I'm leaving you free to pursue a life without such talk. I don't belong where you are, not really. And so this decision is for the best. But if it is any comfort at all to you, during our short time together, you captured my heart. I love you, Oliver.

Eva

"WHERE HAS SHE GONE? I'LL GO TO HER, STOP HER IN HER tracks. What care I for a bit of scandal?"

Algernon eyed him. "Is this the same Oliver I've known my life through? The man who shunned impropriety like a scourge?"

"Yes, it's me. Don't be daft."

"You know what an attachment to such a woman will bring you?"

"Happiness! Great and long lasting happiness."

The duke stared at him for what seemed an entirely long and boorish waste of time before he said, "I think you need to come back to the house with me."

"Will you share with me where she's gone?"

"I believe so, but you might not thank us when we do."

He had no patience for these riddles, so he said nothing, only hurried after the duke to his home.

As soon as they stepped in the door, the duke gave instructions to his butler. "We need to depart within the hour if we're to make the full moon next week."

"Full moon..."

Then the duke ushered him into his office. "Jane has left with Lady Eva and Anna. She has some more items she'd like to pick up before she returns. Oh did I tell you? We are expecting our first child."

"That's wonderful! Congratulations." He waited for the duke to begin making sense once again.

"And so they've left, but we can join them if we hurry. I can't guarantee we'll arrive in the same month, though within thirty days should do the trick."

"Make sense man. I cannot follow this gibberish."

"Don't be concerned. All will be explained on the journey."

He pulled out paper and his ink. "Would you like to write a missive for your mother, let her know you will be traveling, likely gone for two weeks, time to go to Twickenham and back, lingering a week there? Though we could arrange things so that you arrived even earlier if you like. It would be like you'd never left."

Oliver gave up trying to understand and quickly penned a note to his mother and sealed it with the duke's wax and seal. "What shall I do about my trunks?"

"Will you be needing them? Not likely. I'll loan you a few items to get you through the days at Twickenham, and you'll have to pick up some appropriate things when you arrive. Or you won't fit in. I highly recommend a good leather jacket. The women love them."

Oliver followed the duke around while he readied these things, and eventually into his carriage. Once they were finally on their way, Oliver stared him down. "Now. Explain, Algernon. You haven't made a lick of sense since you found me in the park."

"I don't know if I'm the person to be explaining all the particulars."

Oliver waited.

"But I'll tell you what I can. And trust me, you're not gonna believe a word of what I say. You'll just have to trust me until you see for yourself."

Oliver crossed his arms.

"Eva has gone to Twickenham. Remember, where you met her?"

"Of course."

"Those paintings. There's something different about them, do you recall?"

He remembered the strange circumstances of his meeting Eva. The house itself, Nellie, everyone at the ball. "Odd sort of people in that place."

"They're odd for a reason. You see, everyone in those portraits has the ability to travel through time."

Oliver waited for him to laugh or admit to the falsehood, but the duke stared back with the same sincere expression he ever had.

"And Eva is from an entirely different time period. Jane is from the same. Eva's on the run, feels like she's ruined your life, and she is going back to her time period."

"But she hasn't ruined my life. She's made my life everything that is good and interesting and actually real."

"How much is she worth to you?"

"How much…"

"Yes, is it worth it to step into a painting and get sent forward in time to a place you know nothing about, to find her and convince her to come back with you?"

His heart hammered so hard he found it difficult to breathe. As much as he wanted to think the duke had suddenly lost his mind, he appeared as sane as ever. But how could any of the nonsense he was spouting be true?

No matter what was going on, it sounded as though he was on a path to see Lady Eva again. So, he would follow the path until it seemed dangerous to his person. Perhaps that would be the best move?

"Anything is worth being with her again. I need to convince her to stay. My life is an endless boredom with nothing to lighten my path until then. I foresee only misery and obligation and duty, with no joy, love or happiness if we are apart."

"I understand. I remember when I thought Jane was lost to me." As the duke searched Oliver's face, his expression turned calculating. "I'm going to need to explain some things before you go."

"Honestly, I would welcome any further explanation." He hoped the duke would begin to sound like a person not bound for bedlam.

But hours into their carriage ride the duke still hadn't spoken much about where they were headed or what would be required of him or where exactly Eva was.

At last he cleared his throat and leaned forward, his elbows resting on his knees. "Twickenham Manor sits on a line of Fae magic. And the veil between the two worlds is very thin all along the line, but at the very location of Twickenham Manor, there is a crack of sorts, and not all of the magic is on the other side."

"Not on the other side? Meaning there's magic at the manor itself?"

"There is. If you think about it, you noticed it."

He tried to remember his time there. "It was definitely odd. And meeting Eva for a moment only and then she disappeared, that was odd." As he contemplated the whole party, he recognized now, looking back that there was an energy there, a feeling or a hum that coursed through him. "So, you're saying it's magic, Fae magic?"

"Yes, Aunt Nellie. She is the ancient administrator of the magic. She paints the portraits and if you have one, you can travel through time. Anytime."

Oliver sat back on the carriage bench, not believing his ears, but not knowing what else to believe. His story explained a lot about Lady Eva, about the strange words she used when with the duchess. "And you're saying her grace came back in time also?"

"Yes, but I was the first. I traveled to her time and met her there."

"You did?" He searched his old friend's face and saw nothing but honest sincerity.

"Once a month at the full moon, Nellie enables time travel."

"And Eva is traveling there to catch the full moon?"

"She is."

"And we are as well."

"Yes, but there is a chance we will miss it."

At the immediate distress that filled him, Algernon held up his hand. "But do not be concerned. You can travel to her time next month, but arrive the same time she does even if you leave a month later."

Oliver ran a hand through his hair, mussing it in such a manner he would normally be greatly disturbed by how many hairs were out of place. But now, it seemed to fit the general disarray at hand. "I don't know what to think about any of this, but as I see no great harm to my person in attempting it, I am in full support."

"That's the spirit."

"There is a chance we could catch her before she leaves."

"Then that will be the goal moving forward."

He nodded. "But even if you do. You might want to consider the possibility that you'll have to go forward in time just to convince her to be with you."

Oliver did not respond. He couldn't fathom on a real level that anything the duke said was true.

"However, maybe she needs to miss you in her time, and perhaps she would be touched by the gesture and be willing to come back with you."

"Are women from her 'home' all this difficult to win over?"

"I think so. They're raised in a completely different environment. They work. They are independent. Live on their own. They go where they want. Do what they want. And the men have to be really special for them to even want to spend time with them."

Oliver considered his words. "This is what makes Eva so interesting."

"Perhaps. She and Jane were raised to learn and work and grow and become something all on their own, separate from who they marry."

Oliver had never considered such a thing. "Why, that's astounding."

Algernon smiled. "And that response makes me believe you might be just the man for someone like Eva."

They traveled through the night and rested only for the horses. At last, they arrived on the doorstep of Twickenham Manor. "It feels as though I was just here yesterday."

"This place has that effect on everyone. It matters not how long you've been away, it could possibly have been years or a matter of hours. It's all the same here."

Nellie opened the front door before they even knocked. "Oh, I've been expecting you."

They hurried into the front room. Oliver looked in every room they passed. "Is she here?"

Nellie didn't answer but led them into a front parlor.

Algernon smiled. "I have many good memories right here in this room."

"So. You wish to travel through time?" Aunt Nellie eyed Oliver over a pair of glasses. Did she have glasses the last time he saw her? He didn't think so, and he wondered if she even required the use of them.

At any rate, he nodded. "I do. Or rather, what I really want is to be with Lady Eva. Wherever, or whenever she might be." He felt ridiculous, but Aunt Nellie appeared to think everything he said perfectly normal.

"And you understand what's at stake?"

"At stake?"

"That the magic isn't exact. There's a chance you might land on the right day and time or you could be off by a month or year."

"A year?"

"Or two, yes. Though I've been mostly accurate in most cases."

Oliver was feeling less sure. "Is she here still or has she left?"

"She has left."

"What! Did we miss the full moon? Did Jane go with her?"

BACK TO HIS LORDSHIP

"She did. We had a surprise opening in the magic lines as the moon moved into fullness at the very end of the evening, right around early dawn, it was."

Oliver gripped his friend's arm. "Come with me."

"What?"

"Please."

❧ 17 ❦

Eva hugged Anna as soon as she entered the portrait room in the year 2020. "Oh, I'm so glad to see you."

Then Jane hugged them both. "Anna." They rocked back and forth. Eva felt all of her worlds colliding again. Anna had been in both time periods. Jane from the past, Nellie from all the time periods. She looked around and breathed in the smell of delicious modern living. It was good to be home. But even as she said it, a vacant spot in her chest ached. A spot that would never be filled because the only person who would fill that hole had died over two hundred years ago. Her eyes welled up.

"Oh honey, what is it?" Jane reached for her hand.

"I just realized, Oliver, the duke, all of them. They're dead. They've been gone for more than two hundred years now."

Jane's eyes filled with compassion. "Oh, do I remember what that feels like." She pulled her into a hug. "Come on now. It's not as bad as it seems. Now that you know about Nellie and this house, as long as the magic keeps working, he's alive to you. You know?"

Eva shook her head. "No. I don't understand any of it. What have I done?"

"Nothing that can't be fixed, believe me." Anna and her matter of fact personality made Eva smile.

"But come. Before you start wishing for bed pans and leeches, let's go have some fun. I've called the limo, and I'm dying for a good hamburger."

Eva looked down.

"And I've got some clothes, come on."

The three linked arms and took off, Eva determined to rid herself of the vacant loneliness. She was stuck with the absence of the man she loved. What were her options, really? Live in the Regency? In a world where she'd created a complete scandal? With a mother in law who despised her? Or stay here away from all of it, but without Lord Hereford.

She pulled on a pair of Anna's designer jeans and a short cropped shirt. "Are you sure about this?" She yanked on the bottom of her shirt to pull it over the top of her jeans.

Anna laughed. "Oh honey, you have to, in order to get over your newly acquired Regency sensibilities."

She looked at herself in the mirror. She looked great. And she tried to remember what it was like to live and have fun in her time. "You're right. Where are we going?"

"I've called the lords in. We're going to have a party! Remember Lord Smithson was interested before you left? And I've got my Trent…"

"Ah, yes, I do remember. That feels like a really long time ago."

"It was, to you. A month. But to the guys, it was just yesterday."

"Wow, that's crazy."

Jane laughed, spinning in an outfit of tight leather pants and a white shirt. "I love this! I feel so free."

Eva laughed, but a part of her missed the delicate material of her opera gown. She missed the sparkling jewelry, and she missed Beau Brummel and his compliments. She had so many other ideas, so many thoughts about how to spice up the Regency fashion.

And she missed Oliver, how his eyes would not leave her, how intently he watched her, and how he'd so desperately desired to kiss her, but he'd waited.

They piled into the limo, laughing, and told the driver to turn up the music.

"Are we going to the club where we took Algernon?"

Anna nodded. "Yes we are."

"Last time we were here, he and Lord Smithson got in a fight and Algernon spent the night in jail."

"What!"

"Yes, he was coming on to Anna here, and Lord Smithson was not liking that very much, so he swung at Algernon and then got absolutely clobbered." Jane laughed.

"Wait, what! He was coming on to you?" She pointed at Anna and looked between the two of them.

Anna waved her hand. "He's not for me. It worked out just how it was supposed to."

Eva wanted again to know that story. Maybe one day someone would actually tell her how it was Jane that ended up dating the duke, marrying him and living as a duchess in the 1800s.

They pulled up to one of the nicest, most exclusive clubs in London. "Wow, we're already back to London?"

"Oh yeah. Something I completely miss, the ease of travel and communication. Oh, what I would give for a cell phone."

Eva shrugged. "I wonder what would happen if you brought a few towers with you? And two phones."

"And no electricity."

"Oh, right. Again with the electricity."

They hopped out and ran to the front door. Suddenly Eva just wanted to dance and forget her sadness. She wanted to ignore the persistent needling that she'd made a huge mistake. That she would never really be happy until she and Oliver were together.

They followed Anna through the first two rooms and then entered the last, the royals only. The guard let her in on sight and they ran into a much less crowded room.

The guys were in the center of the floor already dancing. "Anna! Eva!" They ran over, and then Lord Smithson shouted. "Jane's back!"

She waved and spun in a circle, and everyone mashed together, bouncing to the beat. Lord Smithson moved close and their bodies touched, moving to the music. She tried not to freak out. Then the music slowed down and Lord Smithson pulled her close without asking. "Let's dance, beautiful."

She laughed. "Okay." But she wasn't entirely comfortable. Thoughts of Lord Hereford and the waltz filled her mind and the magic of her beautiful dress and the way they floated through the ballroom at Almack's together couldn't compare to the mashing loud experience at the London club. She attempted conversation. "So tell me about yourself."

"Right now?" He held her closer.

"Um, okay. Later is fine, I guess."

"I would like to get to know you Eva I've been wanting to for years."

"You have?"

"Of course. You're not over here very much. And last time I was in New York, I don't think you were there."

"Was that the auction?"

"Yes, the very one."

"I heard about it. We donated to the cause. It was for Jane's historical society, wasn't it?"

"Yes. And it's a smashing success now, thanks to all of us. I had a date with a rather elderly woman that lasted too long." He smirked. "But that's all behind us now."

She laughed. "Your sacrifice sounds great indeed."

The music changed back into something with a faster beat, and Eva was grateful to step away and have some space to herself.

They danced and then went out for drinks after, and Eva tried to have fun. She laughed, and truly did enjoy herself now and then, but when it was time to end the evening, she felt only a great amount of relief. They traveled to Anna's estate and the staff showed her to her room.

She stood in the doorway. Her luggage sat in the corner. Her laptop was plugged in on the table. Her phone sat beside it. She opened her drawer and ran her fingers over her socks and underwear. Is this all she wore under her clothes?

She made her way into the bathroom and turned on the faucet, and hot water came after only a moment. She picked up her toothbrush from the holder, filled It with toothpaste and brushed her teeth for about five minutes. Then she turned on the shower. Watching the room fill up with steam, she drew a heart on the mirror.

After her shower, where she washed every part of her twice, she hugged the robe around herself and sat in a chair. She pulled her laptop closer, lifted the cover, and typed Lord Oliver Hereford 1813 England into a Google search bar.

He had a wiki page. She read it and was pleased to learn that he was known for his grove of trees, his goodness to his tenants, and his work as a Whig in the house of lords. The page said nothing about whether he married. And there weren't any children listed. Had he never married?

A great sadness filled her.

She looked up Lady Everly. After much scrolling and searching, she found a picture. She had married, had seven children, four raised to adulthood. And seemed to have lived a happy life. But not with Lord Hereford.

Had he lived out his days in loneliness?

She kept looking. Using the images search, she hoped to find a picture, any, of Oliver. At last, an old image from a book in a digital file showed a smiling Oliver. His hair was white, but he stood strong, his shoulders broad and the familiar twinkle in his eyes made her smile. And miss him. She hugged the screen to her chest. "I'm sorry Oliver."

She noticed red notification numbers on her email. Did she want to dive back into her modern life? Her phone rested upside down on the table top.

She may as well. Even though only a day had passed her email seemed filled with urgent matters. But as she clicked on each one, their complete lack of real purpose surprised her. Was her life filled of a constant stream of meaningless tasks that kept her busy doing nothing?

If she were to base her judgement off this group of emails, she would feel pretty dismal about her purpose in living. She lifted her phone and read her texts.

Her mother remembered she had gone somewhere but not exactly where, then she'd sent pictures of her nephew. He was darling. Work had sent her a couple links to projects. They knew she wouldn't be retuning for another month, but they had reserved a couple clients for her. That was nice. She wondered how much of their treatment of her was dictated by the fact that they hoped her father would one day become a client. Probably all of it. She tossed her phone on the bed and shut her laptop.

Where was the meaning in her life?

She thought back to her time in Regency England. Yesterday. Had her life had meaning there? Not really, but somehow she felt more herself. How odd. And she'd hoped to be able to make a difference there. She'd been so impressed with Oliver, his goodness, integrity. He'd made her want to be better. As she thought about her desires, her actions, she'd been more herself, her best version of herself there with him than any other time of her life.

But how terrible would it be if she'd brought scandal on them both? And how often would she embarrass or scandalize him in front of everyone?

She thought of Jane and Algernon. They managed just fine. In great happiness, actually.

As her head hit her pillow, she closed her eyes and tried to pretend she was back in her bed at the duke's house. Could she make a life for herself there? Perhaps. Did she dare?

That was a question she couldn't answer right now. If the answer came in the morning, she hoped she had the courage to act—whether she would learn to live in her time or travel back to be with Oliver and beg him to be a part of her life.

18

Oliver held his fist up. "Like this?"

"Yep." The duke tapped his own fist into Oliver's. "A fist bump."

"And people do this instead of bowing?"

"Absolutely. They might shake hands as well. That's the more formal greeting, and if you see any lords or prominent business men, then you might shake hands."

"And the ladies?"

"Same." You can shake hands with them. Sometimes we kiss cheeks in a greeting."

"Kiss?"

"Yes, but not like you're thinking. It's a quick peck on the cheek. The ladies do this and sometimes with us gentlemen, too. But they don't do it everywhere. It's just with friends and sometimes those in certain parts of the world. In England where we're going to be, I don't think you'll see much of that. But if Anna or another one of the ladies kisses your cheek, just know it doesn't mean anything."

"And if Eva kisses my cheek?"

"If she does such thing, you're going to have to determine what she means by yourself. I can only get you where she is. After that, you will have to figure out how to woo her on your own."

"I believe I can accomplish such a thing."

"And remember, none of the women wear many clothes."

"They—they don't?"

"No. but you have to remember that it's normal for everyone else. So, try not to notice."

"This is absurd."

"And most of the women wear pants. Breeches. Like the men."

The thought of Eva walking around in breeches made him equally horrified and incredibly enticed.

"You're accepting of the thought of Jane walking around in pants, wearing few clothes and kissing men on the cheek?"

"Of course. The men and women also have very different kinds of relationships. It's something you'll have to talk to Eva about to determine if you and she can come to an agreement."

Oliver was more than confused. "It's just so much information."

They stood in front of a portrait that he was astounded to see had been painted of him and Algernon.

"All we must do is touch this painting?"

"Yes. Now, is there anything small you will be wanting to bring from home?"

He patted his pockets. He had a watch, handkerchief. He could think of nothing else. "No. I have what I need."

"We'll touch it together. Are you ready?"

Oliver almost believed him at this point. "Yes."

They reached out their fingers and touched the paint.

The world swirled around Oliver, and for a moment all he saw was white. Then he found himself on the floor. In the portrait room. With no Algernon in sight. "Your grace?"

But no one answered him. The place was quiet with the thick softness of something ancient.

He walked down the hallway out of the portrait room and everything around him seemed new, but smelled ancient. Like the white stone on a mountain. A beautiful woman approached. And something very familiar nudged him. Something about the woman's eyes, the set of her hair. "Aunt Nellie?"

"Is that what people call me?"

"Yes. But I don't understand. Are you her?"

"Are you looking for the woman who guards this line of Fae power?"

"Yes. And helps people travel through time."

"Oh, I do that also, don't I?"

"Yes, but I think I traveled much farther back than I had planned."

"Well then, let's get you situated."

"Oh yes, please."

She led him back into the portrait room. But this time, there were very few portraits. He couldn't see his own anywhere. "Where did it go?"

"I presume you're talking about your portrait?"

"Yes, of course."

"These all started to appear in this room. They come and go. I'm not sure I have much to do with it."

"Oh, but you do. Algernon said you are the one who paints them."

"And did Algernon tell you how it was he came to be traveling through time?"

"He said his was unconventional."

"Exactly."

"But Aunt Nellie, could you help me return to the year 2020, where Lady Eva has returned? And Jane?"

"I think such a thing is possible."

"You think..."

"These things are not exact, as you have discovered."

"I need them to be a little more exact, if you don't mind. I don't have time for you to think. I need to find Lady Eva."

"Oh, but that's where you are incorrect. You have all the time in the world."

———

A KNOCK AT THE DOOR FILLED EVA WITH A RUSH OF expectation. The butler opened it, and a man's voice called out into the house. "Jane!"

"Algie!"

Eva rushed out into the entry to see the two of them embrace in a reckless abandon. She enjoyed Algernon much more here in this time. Perhaps this was the manner in which they behaved in their home.

When at last they looked in her direction, she laughed. "Algie?"

The duke shrugged. But a certain sadness filled his eyes.

And Eva knew that what she hoped for the minute she saw him, was not to be. "So you are alone."

"I am, but we must go speak with Aunt Nellie at once."

"Why? What has happened?" Jane placed a hand at the side of his face.

"Oliver. He came with me."

"What!" A jolt of electricity shook her hands and suddenly she wasn't sure she could stand on her own. "Is he here?"

Algernon moved forward and offered his arm for her to hold. "We left together. I thought we touched the same painting at the same time, only I was the only one in the portrait room when the world stopped spinning."

"So he changed his mind."

"I think so. But to his credit, he wasn't even entirely certain that I had a fully functioning mind."

Eva frowned. "What did Aunt Nellie say?"

"I couldn't find her. One of the Fae said she was not available at the moment."

"That's not going to work for me." Eva grabbed a set of keys off the front table. "Who's with me?"

Jane rushed to the door. "We all are."

They ran out and hopped into the closest car. Eva beeped the key fob.

"Oh I've missed these carriages. Perhaps we should spend more time here." He eyed his wife. "It's been a long time since I've seen you in breeches. And are these...cow hide?"

"Yes, in this case we just call it leather."

He wrapped a hand around her waist and rested it on her hip. "I like it."

"I could bring them home with us." She stepped up on tip toes and kissed him.

He wrapped his other arm around her. "I'd like that."

"Okay, okay. People. I'm right here."

"Oh, look at our Eva, she's got Regency sensibilities."

"To be honest, I wasn't much of a PDA type gal before I left this century."

"She's perfect for Oliver. I'm telling you." Jane winked.

"Well, where is he?" Now that she'd felt about a thirty second expectation that he would arrive any second, she couldn't wait another hour's time without seeing him. If she must, she'd go back to find him. She clutched her heart. Would she? Go back?

"What is it? Are you well?" Jane rested a hand on her arm.

"Yes. I—I don't know what to think."

"Sometimes in situations such as these, it's best not to think."

"Well someone has to. Because what if Oliver is floating around in time somewhere?"

"Do you think he braved the leap?"

"I don't know, of course, but I think he's not the type to lift his hand to touch a portrait and then change his mind at the last possible millisecond."

"Millisecond?" The duke tilted his head, curious.

"She means, moment."

He nodded.

Jane turned on the car and pulled out. "Oh, I've missed this."

Eva was losing patience with the new duke and duchess. Seemed she much preferred their Regency personae after all.

Did she prefer all people in that era? She might. Everyone here was grating on her every nerve.

And she missed Oliver. The hole in her heart had grown to take over her whole chest cavity, and she wasn't sure how much longer she could bear to be without him.

They pulled up in front of Twickenham Manor. It was only about a mile or two away. She remembered trying to walk the distance and closed her eyes with a smile thinking of Lord Hereford picking her up on the side of the road. How shocked he must have been at her behavior at every turn.

Somehow he'd preferred her to all others. She paused. He'd preferred her even in her shocking behavior.

They rushed into the house without knocking. "Aunt Nellie." Eva called out, not caring how many rules of propriety she broke. Even though they were back in 2020, they were not in America, but she no longer cared. They had to find Nellie and see what was going on with her Oliver.

They ran into the front sitting room. It was empty.

Then Algernon raced down another hallway. "The library. Follow me."

They chased him and pushed open the old thick wood doors. Empty. Not even a maid in sight.

"This home has always been rather odd in its staffing."

"I think they're all Fae."

"They are?" Algernon thought for a minute. "That would explain much."

"How about the portrait room?" Eva shivered. She knew what could happen in that room. Was she ready for such a leap?

OLIVER FOLLOWED THE YOUNG AUNT NELLIE INTO THE portrait room. "So, what can be done? I'm obviously in the wrong time."

She studied him for a moment. "And you wish to follow this woman to 2020, whenever she is, that's where you'd like to be?"

"Yes, please, that's why I touched the painting. I don't know where the duke went. Is he with her?"

She didn't answer. But she walked up and down the row of portraits. A new one appeared where another had held that space on the wall.

"Right there. There he is. And Jane. And Eva. That's her, the woman I'm following."

She pressed her lips together. "But I see no portrait of you."

"Can you make one?"

She considered him. "I could, or we can use the same magical path that brought you here and send you back to your time, to the moment you left."

"But that's not where I'm trying to go."

"It is where, just not when."

"Yes, precisely." He stared about hopelessly hoping his portrait would show up beside the others. When it didn't, he nodded. "Then yes, send me back. From there, I can try again, I presume."

"Yes, you can, as long as you can find me."

He nodded.

"Close your eyes."

He did and felt the soft powdery feeing of snow all around him, followed by the dizzying whirling. His head pounded and he opened his eyes to see he was once again on the floor of the portrait gallery.

He stepped out into the hallway, rushing, clutching his head in an agony. But everything looked different. He was not in his time. And he was not alone.

A man tilted his head to study him. "Have you just arrived?"

Oliver cleared his throat. "Yes. You?"

"Oh no. I never leave. But I've seen many of you come and go." He stepped forward and held out his hand. "I'm Dr. Charles Smithy."

"Oh hello. I'm Lord Hereford, Oliver."

"Ah, a Regency chap, I gather."

"Regency?"

"You're from the time of Prinny as the regent?"

"Yes, of course. And this time is..."

"Much, much later than that. Jumped ahead two hundred years and you've found us."

"Two hundred? Do you know Eva? Or Jane or Anna?"

"I do! All three of those lovely ladies. Have you met Jane, then? Is she making a life for herself?"

"She is, the duchess of Ramsbury. They are some of my dearest friends. And their friend Eva. Have you met her?"

"I did, just recently. She's lovely, quite beautiful. Did she take the leap?"

"Yes, we met in the portrait gallery. And then she disappeared and then showed up again." He waved his hand and then clutched his head, grimacing. "It's all rather complicated."

"I imagine so." He indicated they keep walking. "Let me find something for that headache of yours."

"Oh yes, please. But what do you suggest? A compress?"

"Much better. It's called Tylenol. You're going to love it."

He nodded, interested.

"We don't have much more time of the full moon. I was surprised to see another person show up."

"Can people only take the leap during the full moon, really?"

"So far, that's all I've seen. We should probably let Aunt Nellie know you're here."

"She's the one who sent me."

"But that was Aunt Nellie in the other time period, correct?"

Oliver's brain stopped following. So he just grunted.

The house felt unnaturally quiet. And he saw no one, which he found odd. Didn't a house of this size usually have a full staff of servants? They walked a few more steps when he heard voices.

As they got closer, he smiled. "It's the duke and duchess!" He picked up his feet to run to them. As he reached the stairwell, he met them coming up. "Algernon! Your grace!"

"Oh, call me Jane. You must even when we all return home."

'I'm so happy to see you. I've been a different time, and she thought she was sending me home, but now I'm here.... Where is lady Eva?"

"Oh dear. We thought she was with you."

"What?"

"We sent her back to you. Back to our time." Algernon acted as though it was the safest, most natural thing in the world.

"But you could have sent her anywhere. I would know, having just been in such a place."

"And what are you two still doing here?"

"We have some purchases to make before we go back. We decided to stay the month and then time our return to coincide with Eva's."

"I must go to her." He turned from them, rushing back to the portrait gallery.

"Oliver, chap. It's too late." Algernon's voice irritated him in a deep itch.

"What do you mean, precisely?"

"The full moon is past. You must now wait for the next full moon, and you can return with us to the exact moment she arrives. Trust us, friend. It will seem but a moment for her."

"And I have to stay here thirty days without her?"

Jane smiled.

"Don't smile that doe-y eyed look. I've lived without her already enough."

Jane made a valiant effort not to grin, but he saw it coming and simply walked away. He was in no mood to address the silliness that he knew was coming.

Instead he'd best exert himself to the task of growing accustomed to the idea that he'd be living in essentially a foreign place for the next month, and without Eva.

❧ 19 ❧

Eva spun in the whiteness as her world transformed again. When at last everything stopped, she stood in the portrait gallery. A couple stood across the room and she watched with interest as they both reached forward to touch the paint. With a poof, they disappeared.

Interesting. She'd always wondered how it would appear to others.

"Lord Hereford." She called out into the room, hoping her voice would reach the hallway, if he had wandered out there.

But no one answered.

She made her way to the stairway banister and knew at once she was back in the Regency time period. She looked down at her clothing and gasped. She hadn't changed her outfit. And the duke and duchess had decided to stay for a month. They'd said they'd arrive within minutes of her standing there and would bring her some clothes and other things. But so far, she saw no one, most especially not Oliver, who she'd come back to find.

Perhaps she'd come back to the wrong time. She wandered down the upstairs portion of the home until she found a bedroom. She slipped inside. Perhaps there would be some clothes here she could borrow. It wouldn't do to be seen in her current state, not when she wanted to try to mend her reputation.

She found some clothing and some passably pretty gowns. She reached for the bell pull. How quickly she'd become accustomed to a lady's maid. But in this case, she was entirely necessary. No one could dress in all these clothes by herself.

A short young maid arrived and curtseyed.

"Would you mind helping me dress?"

She nodded. "Certainly." She made no comment about Eva's clothes. Perhaps working here, she saw all kinds of people in every manner of clothing.

"Would you mind terribly helping me know what time it is?"

"It's almost morning miss."

"And what year? What season?"

Her eyes sharpened. And she nodded. "You are in the year 1813. And it is approaching the autumn, miss."

"Thank you." She sucked in her breath. *Months later.* Should she try to go through the painting again?

No, that would be impossible. She'd waited long past the full moon.

She thanked the maid for helping her dress and then determined to find a way to travel to Lord Hereford.

If he hadn't married yet.

As she made her way downstairs, Aunt Nellie left the front room. "Oh, you've returned."

"Yes, can you tell me if Lord Hereford is here?"

"He is not."

She let her shoulders fall. How would she ever be back together with him again?

"He left a full month ago, back to his own estate."

Her heart picked up. "Oh, excellent. Do you know how I might find a conveyance to London?"

"London? If you're hoping to go to Lord Hereford's estate, it is but five miles distance."

Her heart leapt. "Oh is it? Why, that's excellent news." She rested a hand on the banister to keep from falling over. "And would you please help me find a means to travel to his estate?"

"I could call for our carriage, if you like."

"Thank you. I would very much appreciate it."

While she waited for the carriage, she stepped out on the front stoop. The fall weather was chillier than she expected. The trees were all about her. The wall that had been protecting the property was much smaller. But most everything seemed the exact same. She would guess that Twickenham would always remain timeless.

At last a carriage pulled up in front of her, and she allowed a footman to help her up inside.

The more she thought about living in Regency, the happier she was about her situation. She belonged here. The carriage pulled away and she smiled. She found her stays comforting. The skirt that rested against the top of her slippers felt like a beautiful blanket covering her. Her gloves protected her from dirt. They drove down a long lane, lined with trees. The way opened up, and the land spread out in front of her, down rolling hills and rising up again to a stunning large home that sat on a hill at the end of the lane.

They continued down the drive while Eva drank in everything around her. Until at last they stopped at the front stoop of what she hoped was Lord Hereford's home.

She waited until the footman came around to open her door. The housekeeper and the butler had come to stand out in front.

When she stepped out to greet them, another woman approached—older. Lord Hereford's mother.

Eva curtseyed.

Lady Hereford did the same. "You must be Lady Eva?"

"I am."

She studied her for a half breath and then she held out her arms. "Come here, child. We are so happy you've finally returned."

Shocked at the woman's sudden support, Eva didn't need to be told twice. She stepped forward and then hesitantly into Lady Hereford's arms.

"I came as soon as I could."

The woman's seemingly frail arms gifted her with a strong embrace.

"Mother? Who is it?" Lord Hereford's voice felt like honey to a parched throat.

She felt his gaze, felt his halted progress. She turned. And then drank him in. He stood tall, strong. His eyes held their same kindness. His smile, growing in delight looked the same. It couldn't have been too long since they'd last seen each other.

"You've come back."

"Yes, I have. Back to your lordship." She grinned at her own movie reference. Which no one would understand except her. But that didn't matter, because her earl was standing right in front of her, smiling and happy to see her. "I wonder if it's not too improper of me to come call on you..."

"Alone."

"Oh, quite. Yes. Alone." She'd done it again.

"I would expect nothing less." He chuckled then he held out his hands. "Come here, you."

For a moment, she had to look around to make sure they were in the correct time period.

"What?"

"How long you plan to make a gentleman wait?"

She stepped forward. "I guess not much longer?"

"Darn right." He reached for her hand and led her away, through the front room, through the study, past the sitting room and into the library. All the while her expectation growing. And her wonder. Had he come to her time period after all?

When at last he stopped, shut the door, and then pulled her into his arms. "I've missed you."

"I didn't think I could survive another minute without you." She stood taller.

"So how about that last item on your list?"

"Only if you know what it means."

"Oh, I know what it means. Do you?"

"I do."

His eyebrow rose in an adorable sort of way. Something about him had changed, a different kind of confidence, an element of fun. And she liked him even more.

He searched her face in one delicious slow motion. His eyes lingering on her lips, before moving up to her own. The love that stared back from him was beautiful, constant, and true. She could lose herself forever in the loyalty she saw staring back at her. "I love you, Eva."

"And I love you, too, my lord." She'd come back for him. She'd go anywhere for him. Life was only meaningful if he was in it.

As his gaze once again lowered to her mouth, he pressed his lips to hers in an agonizing intensity. He kissed her again and again, exploring every angle. His arms wrapped around her back, holding her closer, cradling her against him.

She returned the urgency for more of her own and their kisses turned insistent. She pressed again and again, pulling at him, asking, needing, until he scooped her up in his arms and brought her to the couch. But with her on his lap, he slowed their intensity, pausing for a moment to look into her eyes. "Marry me."

"Yes. When? Soon? Now."

He laughed in a quiet belly sort of way and then kissed her once more, twice. "Are you here to stay, then?"

"Yes. And may I never see another portrait room again."

"You'll hear no argument from me there. Whatever you need, Jane can bring it back for you."

"Is this really happening?"

"It really is."

His face shone with his love for her, and she wasn't sure how she could be any happier. "Thank you for coming back. I love you, my Eva, my American newly penniless heiress from San Diego, California."

She gasped. "How could you..."

"And don't worry, I've asked your father. He fully supports the match."

"What?"

"And little Joey says hi, and he wants you to have this." He reached inside his pocket and pulled out a match box car.

She lifted the car from his hand. And then tipped back her head and laughed. "Tell me all about it later." Then she tipped back his head and lowered her mouth to his. "I'm not nearly finished."

He smiled beneath her mouth, wrapped his arms around her more tightly and dipped her to his side where she was more soundly kissed than she ever had been with plans to continue every day for the rest of her life.

THE END.

READ Jen's other Time Travel Regency HERE.

20

CHAPTER 1 DATING THE DUKE

A s soon as the airplane doors opened, Jane was the first to get off the plane. She raised her hands in the air and walked down the nearly empty exit ramp. *Victory.* She made her way to baggage and felt a smile stretch across her face when a driver held up a sign with her name on it. "Lady Jane."

She collected her bags and the driver took her to Chatwick Manor. Driving back across the same countryside she had travelled when she journeyed back to Regency England just a few weeks ago brought back all the familiar anticipation. But she told herself, she was not hopping two hundred years this trip, she was going to relax in the year 2019. So there was nothing to feel anxious about.

Actually standing in the Regency time period had been surreal. She had hurried so that there would not be the temptation to stay, gave herself just enough time to deliver her message, sign agreements, grab a memento and go. She smiled as she fingered a slip of ribbon. *1817 ribbon.*

And she had celebrated when she made it back without weakening in her resolve, without seeing Algernon. Oh, it hadn't been easy. She had hungered for him, her hands shaking with hope that somehow he would have guessed her intent and would be standing at Twickenham Manor waiting to hold her in his arms. But no. He had an estate to save, caves to ravage, and a wife to find. She couldn't stand in where she did not belong any more in his life. She grinned to herself, thinking of the pictures Anna took of his discovery of the caves.

When she pulled up in front of Chatwick Manor, she wasn't surprised to see Lady Anna. They had only recently become close, the woman had a hard time getting over the fact that Jane was born a commoner. But since her last visit, when Jane literally saved her estate, Anna had taken to texting and conversing with her as old friends.

As soon as the driver opened Jane's door, Anna squealed. "I just found out I own a foundation."

Jane laughed. One of the interesting parts of Anna travelling during the smuggling find and visiting the caves was that when she returned home, she could see the changes that had happened all around her situation. "I saw Algie has increased his holdings as well."

"Yes," she waved her hand, unconcerned as ever with the plight of others. "I help with literacy now too, and I'm thrilled about it. It's amazing, Jane, what you did for our family."

Jane smiled. She at last felt at peace about the way she left things with Algernon. His estate was famous around the world for the good it did, stating its reasons stemming from two hundred years ago when the Duke of Shelton set out the expectations for their family and its wealth. By his own dukely decree, they were to share ten percent of their fortune always, forever. "I'm even more happy about helping you all than I am about saving our historical society and my own dissertation." She laughed and then air kissed Anna on the cheeks.

They hurried inside, arm in arm, and Anna told her all about the plans for that evening. Jane was not quite the partier that Anna was, but Charles would be there and she was excited to hear what he would do with all of the research she had forwarded on to him. After her big splash so strongly proving the strength of this family of daughters, he couldn't very well come out and try to prove the opposite. But she couldn't be sure. So she wanted to discuss their research, which she knew Anna would find incredibly boring.

Jane laughed at something Anna said. "How is Trent?" What an unusual turn of events. Never would she have guessed that Trent and Anna would even hold the slightest interest in each other, ever, but here they were, bouncing back and forth across the ocean to spend time together.

"He's lovely and fits right in with everyone. You won't care if he comes, will you?"

Jane shook her head. "No, I'm way beyond Trent."

"True." She sighed. "I imagine, once you've won Ramsbury's heart…" She wiggled her eyebrows.

"Now that's just cruel." But she couldn't help smiling even if it was awful to act as though they had even the tiniest modicum of a chance together.

"Oh, come now, the full moon is in just a few more days."

"And?"

"Well, and..." She stopped, and grabbed both of Jane's hands and stared into her eyes, her expression, daring, sparkling, full of challenge. "You should go back. And this time, spend some time, at least a month."

Her heart skipped and pounded and she had to place a hand at her chest to remind herself to breathe. "But what good would that do?" Her face started grinning before she could even stop herself. "I can't stay forever..."

"Can't you?"

No, how could she just up and leave her time? Her century? But, to see Algernon again, a whole month in Regency England? She didn't know if she could resist such a thing.

Anna squealed. And Jane had never seen her behave so... normally. "You are totally doing this! Oh! I want to come! But I can't this go round, that last travel made my head ache for weeks."

Jane didn't care what it did to her head. Now was the perfect time for a vacation. And especially one where no one would notice she had gone. But did she dare? The more she thought about it, the more she knew she just might.

21

CHAPTER 2 DATING THE DUKE

Algernon approached the entrance to Twickenham Manor. To think, three months ago, he had never cared to enter the smaller manor, and here he was arriving for the third time in so many months at their front door.

It swung open, a young man running down the drive, shouting back over his shoulder, "I'll return at the full moon."

Algernon shook his head. Would he ever be surprised about what he found at Twickenham? He suspected not.

He peeked into the hallway. This time, the house was bursting with people, all in costume. It appeared to be a masquerade ball. Well, this certainly complicated things. All he wanted was a word with Nellie, and a possible visit to see Jane. If he dared. Which he might. But he had to be absolutely sure he could return. So much was at stake now for his estate. Perhaps if he travelled to Jane, he could convince her...dare he even hope...dare he even put to words his thoughts? Convince her to come back with him. Yes. He had to try. He wanted Jane in his life.

He pushed through the crowd, everyone in masques. He grabbed the nearest person, "Have you seen Nellie?" The masqued guest shrugged.

People would point in a general direction and he would follow. A woman stepped closer. "Oh, your grace. I'm so happy to see you again." Her voice sounded familiar, older, but he couldn't place it. She giggled and nudged the lady at her side. "I won him, fair and square one evening. Fifty thousand dollars."

He gasped. The woman at the auction? But she moved past, greeting people all around her. At last he thought he saw the back of Nellie's white hair. He moved in that direction. But a woman stood in his way, in costume. "It's me. Lady Anna."

From his time. "Oh, Lady Anna, I just want to see Nellie. I've got to go back to Jane."

"Come with me." She led him in the opposite direction he'd seen Nellie go. Many called to Lady Anna as they passed and she waved cheerfully back in response.

"Who are all these people?"

"Those who are about to travel or who have been. Nellie invites a group of us every full moon." She moved the masque away from her face. "I don't think she's expecting you."

"No, she wouldn't be. Does it matter? I would very much like to go back to see if I can convince Jane to..." He swallowed. "Live here."

"Let's get you on your way."

"Can you do that?"

"Well, no, but I can at least get you in the right place."

They walked up the stairs, and it gradually quieted. Algernon appreciated leaving the loud chatter behind because he needed to think, to concentrate.

They took another set of stairs further up into the house. Lady Anna said, "So we'll go back into the painting room, you'll have to show me which one is yours."

He opened his mouth to express his confusion when Nellie joined them. "Hello, your grace. Thank you Lady Anna. I'll take it from here."

She smiled. "Good luck Algie. You deserve to be happy."

He smiled a nervous half smile. Now that Nellie was here, he felt more anxious than he had expected. Going to another time accidentally was one thing, but purposefully travelling again seemed quite a different degree of brave altogether.

"You, of course, haven't been up here yet. This is where most people come and go through time."

"Do they do it differently than I have been?"

"Most do, yes, they enter through their paintings usually."

"So, I could do that now, enter through a painting and go back?"

She nodded. "You could."

"And if I convince Jane, could you bring us both back to this time again?"

"I can. More or less."

"More or less? Is that a yes or a no?"

She ignored him and opened up the door to what looked like an enormous art gallery. He followed her in, mouth open at all the different portraits. He could only guess they had all travelled through time. Some day he wanted to sit this woman down and get some answers. But he suspected you only got the answers she cared to give, when she wanted to give them. She led him to a mirror, tall, it reached to the ceiling, and she left to get his painting.

She brought over a large canvas and uncovered it. But in doing so, a huge flash of light filled the room and grew in intensity right around the mirror. He thought it would be hot, but it was cool. He hesitated to look right in its center, but found that he could, without any trouble. He was filled with a yearning to enter this light. Everything else in the room was invisible to him, as if the light consumed it all. He stepped closer, staring. A figure started small, at the back of the light and moved toward him. The light flashed with a greater intensity, not brighter, not hotter, just more, and the figure moved closer. Jane!

He rushed to her, met her in the center of the light. It lifted the ends of his hair, filled his body with energy but all he focused on was Jane. He pulled her into his arms. She felt soft against him. And she smelled amazing. He buried his face in her hair. "Jane, my Jane." The light flared all around them, blocking out anything but the two of them.

"Algernon. I came to you."

"Wait, you did? I thought I came to you."

They looked around. Jane wrinkled her lovely nose and he had the strongest desire to kiss it. And then her. "Then where, or I guess, when, are we?"

He pulled her close. "When would you like us to be, Jane? I can't live without you."

She looked up into his eyes, put a hand at the side of his face, and said, "Wherever you are. I'm here for a month, maybe forever."

"Make that forever, Jane. If you will, if you can leave all in your time, I will make you a Duchess, give you as many ball gowns as your heart desires and teach you every tiny Regency detail you've been wondering about."

Her eyes widened, and he hurried to continue before the fear crept in.

"But even more, I will love you, Jane. I will treasure you and hold you as something precious to me, for as long as we both live. I want you at my side Jane, will you marry me?"

She choked, the light around them continued, and then she searched his face. "Yes. Oh yes! Algie, I will marry you."

The light doused. And they stood in Nellie's upstairs room.

"That took you long enough. I've been standing here trying to decide to what time I was sending you both." Nellie stood with hands on her hips, both paintings at her feet.

"Nellie!" Jane smiled. "I just left you in 2019 and here you are. I won't try to understand how."

She held up her hands. "Just enjoy each other. Come back if you ever want to go back to your birth time, Jane, grab a hotdog on Fifth and Broadway." She winked and then left the room.

Their eyes followed her out of the room. Then Algernon turned his attention back to the precious woman in his arms. "Did you just agree to marry me?"

Her face broke into a huge smile. "I did."

He ran a thumb along her lower lip. "I couldn't be happier, Jane. If you're sure..."

She stood up on tiptoes and reached up to grab the back of his neck. His heart thrilled when he felt the pressure of her soft lips on his. He mumbled against her mouth, "MMM. Welcome to Regency England Lady Jane Sullivan." Then he responded to her searching with an insistence of his own, angling his mouth to capture the most of hers he could, over and over, pulling her up against him, thrilling with the thought that the Jane he thought he'd lost was back and had agreed to be his. "Mm. Wait. I have a confession to make."

She tipped her head. "What?" Her lovely eyebrow rose in a delicious arc he wanted to kiss back down into place.

"I got a tattoo."

Her mouth opened wide, wider than he'd ever seen it go. "You what!"

"I did. I can't show you now, it's in one of those places, but I will, that is, when I can, when we are..."

"Married?" She laughed. "I cannot believe it. Was this when you were out with Anna?" A slight dissatisfaction crossed her eyes. Which he hurried to erase. "No! Of course not. I just got sent to prison when I was out with them, no, me and The Band of Brothers got matching tattoos, 'Band of Brothers.'"

She held a hand to her head. "I really cannot believe it. I'm tempted to take a picture of it for posterity's sake just to freak out all the historians of my day."

"Henry the fifth, you know."

"Yes, I know." She shook her head, stepped back and took a good look around the room. Then she squealed, running to the window. "I'm here. Last time I could not appreciate it properly."

"Oh, last time. Jane." He followed her and reached for her hand. "I thank you. You have saved my estate." Then he grinned. "Well, I suppose it's fitting for it will now be our estate. Jane, you've saved your own estate, and the estate for our children." He pulled her close again and her eyes widened with such a look of love and hope he couldn't help but press his lips to hers all over again. "I love you, Jane."

"And I love you too, Algernon."

READ the rest of Dating the Duke HERE.

FOLLOW JEN

Follow her Newsletter
www.jengeiglejohnson.com

Jen's other published books

Back To His Lordship
Regency Time Travel

The Nobleman's Daughter
Two lovers in disguise

Scarlet
The Pimpernel retold

A Lady's Maid
Can she love again?

Spun of Gold
Rumplestilskin Retold

Dating the Duke
Time Travel: Regency man in NYC

Charmed by His Lordship
The antics of a fake friendship

Tabitha's Folly
Four over protective Brothers

To read Damen's Secret
The Villain's Romance

Follow her Newsletter

Copyright © 2019 by Jen Geigle Johnson

All rights reserved.

No part of this book may be reproduced in any form or by any electronic or mechanical means, including information storage and retrieval systems, without written permission from the author, except for the use of brief quotations in a book review.

www.ingramcontent.com/pod-product-compliance
Lightning Source LLC
Chambersburg PA
CBHW061217170626
46809CB00007B/2510